# LIGHT THERE IS TO FIND

# Light There is to Find

A novel
by

## HEATHER ROUNDS

Adelaide Books
New York/Lisbon
2018

LIGHT THERE IS TO FIND
A novel
By Heather Rounds

Copyright © by Heather Rounds

Cover design © 2018 Adelaide Books

Published by Adelaide Books, New York / Lisbon
adelaidebooks.org

Editor-in-Chief
Stevan V. Nikolic

For any information, please address Adelaide Books
at info@adelaidebooks.org
or write to:
Adelaide Books
244 Fifth Ave. Suite D27
New York, NY, 10001

ISBN-10: 1-949180-46-8
ISBN-13: 978-1-949180-46-6

Printed in the United States of America

*What you need to know is very little, but to know*

*that little takes very very much.*

— G.I. Gurdjieff

# 1

# *Washington D.C. to Yerevan, Armenia*

After the Paris layover, a pastor from Sarasota, Florida sitting across the aisle told me everything he wanted me to know about Armenians. How beautiful they are, how smart and educated and jobless, how the men have hearts that give out by 55.

"The biggest problem with Armenians," he said, "is nobody has money. They need so much. And they have so much to give. Tragic."

The pastor told me how he married an Armenian woman he met online, the granddaughter of a leader in the Azerbaijan war and former mayor of the town of Gyumri. I told him Gyumri was where I was headed and he cocked his head to the side with quiet theatrics, then wrote an address on his cocktail napkin and handed it to me.

"When you get there, go talk to my wife's family over at Tolstoy #24. I mean that's what's so great is you *can*. They'll take you in no questions asked."

The pastor told me how he sponsored an Armenian orphanage and periodically went over to check in. In Sarasota, in addition to his church work, he ran a dry cleaners and kept a little bucket on the counter to collect money for supplies he sent back to the kids. At the orphanage, the ones who arrived with no surnames got a name that translates into son-of-bird.

"Makes more sense in their language," he said.

His big advice: "Don't be too quick to smile. Don't smile too fast like an American. You know how we are! They're going to be kind to you but standoffish at first. They'll size you up. A young American woman travelling alone is rare. Let them take their time to sniff you out first and then you'll see they'll be your best friends. They'll break right open for you."

He adjusted his neck pillow, closed his eyes. "I'm surprised you would go," he said as he faded off. "Strange choice for a vacation."

A sliver of me wanted to say, *Yeah I'm surprised, too*. I kept silent, though, let his talking taper off. He'd lost me with the online wife thing, but regardless, I just wanted to be as alone as I'd left home to be.

The plane jittered with the back and forth of mothers working to appease tugging children. Square-jawed, gray-headed men in tweed coats and hats stood in the aisle. The Armenian language fluttered over me. A collection of buoyant, undecipherable sounds massed together in the air like one collective conversation. Everyone seemed to know everyone else. Everyone seemed to have boarded together, and in four hours they would all pour out the airport exit together. All glad to be home.

I swallowed another Xanax and lifted the window shade to a gauzy sky, the land fading to patches of dry brown and gray rock thousands of feet below. Somewhere in the fuzz between wake and sleep, I waited to get where I'd told myself to go.

--

Call it a strange choice for a vacation, but I'd intended to see the sun there. And a building. One specific building, with the sun hitting it. A building in a photograph that lived on the wall of Narine's Armenian bakery in Washington D.C.. A photograph I'd seen for years.

I'd told myself, I just wanted the sun hitting that specific building. And I just wanted the sun hitting me as I stood next to that building. And I wanted to set up my easel and paint it as it happened. On that plane, rushing away from my life, I told myself that my wants were a tidy and simple package.

He hadn't asked for an explanation but even if he had I wouldn't have said any of that to the pastor from Sarasota, Florida. Other than telling Narine, I hadn't explained anything to anyone. Other than her, nobody knew where I was headed. Nobody knew I was leaving.

I thought: *What's there to explain to a pastor from Sarasota, Florida?*

--

I'd turned to art early, committed myself in a half-ass way.

Growing up in Alamogordo, New Mexico, my family lived at the thinnest point of a thinning highway beyond a standard air force base checkpoint, in a standard air force base duplex. The days were always too bright and the nights a flat purple.

When he was home from mysterious flights in his F-15, my father would doodle with pencil and paper. He'd sit on the porch or in his favorite chair in the living room and make caricatures of my younger sister Frannie and I, and occasionally my mother when she didn't demand he stop.

He'd encourage me to draw, too. He never showed me technique, I was probably too young for that anyway, but he was good at supporting the act itself.

"By drawing things you can remake them," he told me once. He was drawing my toddler sister who was playing in the yard in a sand pile, he gave her elongated horns and I laughed.

"It's a power," he'd said. "To freeze something. Make it live forever the way you want it."

Of course, this is the sort of thing you say to a five-year-old, to make it seem more mystical than it is, or just to keep them occupied. But it appealed to me, this practice, this idea of freezing something and carrying it away.

"You got the knack," my father had said. I had something, a skill he'd passed into my blood.

After my father stopped being, and my sister and mother and I carried on our lives in Maryland, I relied all the more on the skill in my blood.

I'd decided early on that I wanted to be a painter. I preferred landscapes and unpopulated settings. I relied on color to make up the structures that fell in my path. Familiar bridges. Grassy acreage lining the city's gray. Maybe some light twinkling on the surface of water in the night. On a handful of occasions, I sold what I made.

But the money that came came rarely, and so, at thirty-two years old, I let my day job—that gray mass of hours spent in a windowless office—take up the bulk of my time. I wasn't much in the habit of making things live forever the way I wanted them to be.

--

Before Armenia, when I daydreamed about what it might look like to run away without telling anyone, it looked something like pulling my car over on the way to work, hopping the highway guardrails, running through the dense evergreens, and finding a rolling pasture on the horizon that would swallow me whole.

None of it ever looked like the queue for boarding a plane, anxiety medication and credit card debt from flights and accommodations. I'd never daydreamed about that sort of experiment in movement. But then there are pivots sometimes. Things force you to look new directions, feel out new edges.

It happened during that gray mass of hours, in that windowless office, when the architecture of my body failed and I tumbled down from my chair, stirring to confusion with a whale-sized cry. A bloom of red filled my eyes, like that hot spot that takes over your vision when staring at the sun. The spot went from red to violent white. Then came the tingly blackout that comes with pain. Then the hard light over a hospital bed.

I thought, *this is death, this whiteness.*

--

I was the host of a rare disease. Thirty-two years of abnormal development. The kind of tumor they sometimes call a *homunculus*, the Latin term for the phrase *little man*.

The doctor said, smiling, "We call them that because they're all covered in hair, teeth and nails. Little monsters."

The way I remember the doctor explaining it, I came from a womb composed of fragile cells. And from the beginning the little man took to claiming my fragile cells as its own. Taking advantage of my weak terrain, it clutched up inside me and gradually organized itself over the course of my life. I was the terrarium, the right ecosystem, the right blend of moister and heat for disease.

The little man and I were born together, but we grew at different paces, into different beings. And as I took shape, as my limbs stretched and articulated and I went about my life, the little man camped out in a crook of my fallopian tubes, quietly swelling and twisting. A fatty chunk in a dark corner, growing its own hair and teeth. A complete evolution.

The little man first presented itself to me as a dull pressure on the left side of my abdomen. Then, as a small, ignored lump. And then eventually, a rupture came from under my pelvis and I knew I was not alone in myself.

The little man, black, toothy, hairy and gripping. The little man deep inside and discovered by way of emergency. The little man suctioned out. Complete resection. Classified as a zero in the system of cancer staging. Benign. A zero. Incapable of metastasis.

Staring down at me on the cold white bed, the doctor offered his most professional smile. I don't remember if it helped but I understood that that's what it was designed to do. The structured, congratulatory smile doctors reserved for such moments of reporting non-fatality to patients. Of announcing you've lived because you might not yet believe it. A doctor's professional smile, followed several breaths later, once it was clear I had no further questions to ask, by the smile's slow fade and some words: "We should tell you that you won't be able to conceive."

--

Outside the Yerevan airport the evening sky glowed the purple-blue of a new bruise and dust and exhaust hung dense in the hot air. A slight framed man with kind eyes stood next to a Mercedes and waved my way. I waved back and he sprung toward me saying what I took to mean he could drive me where I needed to go. I said the name of the hostel I'd booked and he said something else.

"English?" I asked.

He took a pad of paper from his pocket and wrote out a price I hadn't the mind to convert into an understandable sum. I turned my mouth down to say the number seemed a little steep, which I assumed it was, and he crossed it out and wrote out a slightly lower number beneath it. I nodded okay, with some slight hesitation to the gesture, as though to say I was giving in easy, but I knew I could have hung in for a lower price. He reached for my luggage and I mimed resistance but gave in easy, letting him carry one of my bags, unsure what custom would say to do. On his forearm was a tattoo that looked like a pen stroke smudged with water.

A man and woman were already in the car. I climbed into the back with the woman and both greeted me with broad smiles. The three of them chattered as we left the airport. At first I took them to be friends or family, then noticed the woman had a small suitcase at her side and realized they were probably paying for a ride, too.

The woman flashed me a steady stream of toothy smiles— smiles that held the affection of an attentive grandmother, smiles hard to keep up with. We passed a small fender bender on the side of the road and she clicked her tongue and flashed me a look that said, *can you believe that?* I smiled and shook my head to confirm I was seeing what she was seeing.

The road was lined with storefronts, watermelon stacks, trash clusters and colorful bits of plastic strewn around the traffic islands like the aftermath of a music festival. Men sat on rice bags. Road signs were all in Armenian script. An ancient, beautiful lettering that most of the world, myself included, would never bother to learn.

We took a turn into an apartment complex and when the car stopped and everyone turned to me, I assumed we'd arrived at the hostel. The driver jumped up, took my belongings and stacked them delicately on the ground, pointing to the entrance. He got back in his Mercedes and all three waved. I waved back. The woman turned in her seat to look out the back window as they turned the corner and disappeared, her white teeth glowing in the dark.

I rung the bell below a taped up paper sign that read: HOSTEL HERE RING BELL. Back came the buzzing and the click of the loosened door. I climbed the stairs to the lobby and found a pimpled boy behind a desk computer. Stirring to his feet, his voice buckled, "Yes hello okay."

I explained who I was and he explained to me in some semblance of my language, enough to cling to at least, the prices, cleaning hours, kitchen rules, finishing the introduction by pointing to the bathroom and then to my reserved room, the only private room at the hostel—windowless, barely the size of a walk-in closet, a cot sized bed covered in a neon green sheet, maybe satin, under a wide faced clock and a ceiling fan.

Hostel Boy backed out of the room and I clicked the fan on, thankful it worked. I wondered, not yet tired, what to do next. The clock said it was nearly 8 p.m.. I opened the door and Hostel Boy leaped up from his seat.

"I would like to go out," I told him.

"Yes there is much go. Yes. Just back by maybe 2. Yes, of course."

I descended the stairs, back out into the hot night and walked along the wide, carless road. On the corner two men sat on logs hunched over a chessboard, beside a watermelon stand. Rinds of melon lay strewn around them on the sidewalk. Their eyes met mine, blank and wide, and I walked by casual, chin up, as though to say I knew the way, as though to say that the road was nothing new for me, and beyond any doubt I knew what I was doing.

But the weight of their expressions and the dark of night settling in and the shuttered stores said I had come at the wrong hour. And then the passing woman concentrating on the meaty bone she'd grabbed from the sidewalk, the breast she flashed out as she wrapped the discarded rib or leg of something in her shirt. That was another signal. So, I turned back to the hostel realizing I'd better try it again in the conventional safety of morning.

--

That first night under the lime green sheet with the fan spinning above, I ran my hand over my stomach. I thought I felt a twinge and was gripped by a fleeting worry that I'd damaged something the surgery had tried to mend with the stress of the travelling. But that gave way to a different worry. I dwelled on my explanations, what I might say when it came time to answer to those I hadn't bothered telling I was leaving.

I lay there resenting what the pastor from Sarasota had said. I lay there and hated him for perpetuating the stigma that says it's strange for women to travel alone. For pivoting my gaze to an idea I didn't want to apply to myself.

*Strange.*

*Why can't it not be strange?*

I said it loud for nobody. I swallowed a Xanax and closed my eyes.

--

After they suctioned the little man from my fallopian tubes, I woke blistered, my throat rubbed raw from tubes, riding the waves of dizziness and farting out carbon dioxide. I fingered the skin around the incision and felt the sting of broke tissue. The incision itself, through which they'd sucked out the little man, was well-shrouded in a band-aide dome. And the skin around it, itchy, lumpy, bruised. An ache stretched up through my shoulders. The stinging, the farting, the bruising. I'd been well warned of what my body might do and it was doing all of it. So, I let it be. I kept my spine pressed into my mattress, and my palm rubbing the bandage glued to my incised gut. I molded to the dull achy weight and didn't leave my apartment for days.

But it wasn't so much physical pain that kept me confined. That mostly waned fast. What stayed was a static in my head and a general lack of motivation. What stayed was my remaining problem, which sustained my fresh attention by continually morphing into something else.

At first the problem presented itself as an emptiness. I would never conceive. I'd always played the role of creator of worlds in my own life, and it hadn't hit so much in the hospital, but at home, with nothing but time, I thought of this hollowness packed into my otherwise healthy body.

But then I concluded that it was not because of infertility that I felt hollow. I had, after all, spent my whole life cradling the tiny man inside me, and I wondered if it was his absence that made me feel empty. Besides, I'd never concerned myself much with the idea of having children. And now with it presented as a non-option I found myself unfazed. I imagined the hollowness to be lightness, I experimented with accepting my fate.

Then I saw my barren landscape, my empty uterus and mangled fallopian tubes as signals to change my life somehow. But change felt like too abstract a thing, there in my bed. The light feeling went hollow again, the way dark thinking takes hold of you when you wake in the night. And so my problem became hate. I took to hating my empty uterus and mangled fallopian tubes, my job, my boyfriend, my non-existent art career. I had no true definition.

Not unusual. Surgical recovery can bring an emptiness and sour emotions. A patient needs time to regain themselves, to reconnect with what they were before their body underwent involuntary change. But if one allows the body to stay stagnant too long, recovery can backfire. The air spoils and the nights get longer. For some days I didn't fight the backfire.

Then a morning came when I woke, twisted my torso to rise up and realized I could hear my bones. A clank in my knee crook and the small of my back, a metallic sound. There was a pain, too, in moving at certain angles.

The pain I curbed with pills but the noise remained. Weren't these noises that had always been there, though? Wasn't it just that, with all the quiet of the situation, I heard myself from inside out? The only sounds I'd been listening to were the intermittent vibration of my ignored phone, buried under a floor of laundry.

To cut the sound, I rose up and opened the window next to my bed, letting in some of the world's noise and light. A good first step, I thought. In the window a spider rolled around a strand of web. From its body came the thin thread, gently batted by the breeze, sometimes conforming to the shape of the web but more often just twirling and hanging. When the threads failed to land where they belonged, the spider ate them, taking its work back down to the abdomen, absorbing the proteins. And then it tried again.

I never thought what thin chance a web has. Falling silk constantly in battle with the wind.

For two days I watched the spider more than I didn't. At night I closed the window and each morning I opened the window and the spider was there. I took some photographs, thinking I'd paint it in the future. It was not a time for productivity. I had a head of dull static and a belly of gauze. Still, I embraced the activity of watching the spider. It was a small way to live, but it was living and it was mine.

Eventually, though, came the knock on my door. Frannie's calls—like so many others'—had gone unanswered for long enough. I cracked the door. At the sight of her face, a dizziness, a whirl began in the dark of me.

--

"Self-alienation, Sara." said Frannie, diagnosing me with something she'd diagnosed me with often.

My sister Frannie. The younger sister, but labeled more mature. The bigger boned sister of better posture and a surer voice.

We had a long-established choreography: I allowed my little sister a slight foothold in pedagogy, a foothold that I granted but gracefully ignored while swallowing back the queasy sensation her presence so often left me with.

I let Frannie lure me into the harsh brightness of day with promises of baklava and Armenian coffee, around the corner at Narine's Bakery. As we walked there, still in my narrow tunnel world, the swish of the cars came up like rogue waves and the sidewalk, its people jetting out from everywhere, presented impossibilities.

At the bakery I twirled the coffee mud at the bottom of my cup and said, "There is this spider I want to paint. In my window."

Frannie reminded me that self-alienation is when you distance yourself from you and everything about you. She tore away a piece of my untouched baklava. "I told mom about the surgery, just so you know. Have you talked to Eric yet? He's been calling. Call him."

I said, "Hey, where do you think that photo was taken? I've always wondered." I pointed above the table to a photo of an anemic shell of a concrete building, bolted to a dry plain in the sunshine, a totally washed out pallet of yellows and whites.

Frannie said, "Kind of looks like New Mexico, doesn't it? You should ask about it. It's good to be curious."

The photo hung crooked against the wall. Over the last four years, I'd watched the cheap plastic frame take on a thickening coat of dust and slump slightly further to the left. Abandoned in plain, bright sight.

*It's good to be curious.*

So I walked up to the counter and asked, "Where was that picture taken?"

I asked sheepishly and with all the frailty I had to present. I asked in a thin voice that said: *Please answer my questions because I'm trying to put something back in me. I'm scraped clean and raw to the touch.*

The question crawled slowly from my throat. Just hung in the air. Narine looked up at me, a woman of solid smiles, patient steady face and striking, heavy black eyes. A woman's face I had come close to so often for snaps of throwaway time. She looked startled at first. Despite my frequent visits, despite my time standing across the counter from Narine, I'd felt no real need to say much to her. What was there to say?

Narine brushed away some sugar from the countertop and answered my question.

# 2

A Russian couple stood in the kitchen eating breakfast in their underwear, ignoring me as I passed to the bathroom. I showered fast, and made my way outside, where the day waited bright and old women sold pastries from a small box made of fogged-over Plexiglas. I stuck out my index finger, made the symbol for one, pointed to a pastry. A buttery, perfectly heart-shaped pastry.

I picked a direction and walked, chewing the perfect pastry, hoping to find the town center. I took note of how I felt. Nothing barren or empty in me, nothing matted, balled and heavy. My insides felt baseline. The outset. That first walk on that first morning when I could have walked for miles and miles.

Nothing was as it had been the night before in Yerevan. Roads were jammed with wheezing, break-squealing traffic, sidewalks were lined with cones of flowers stacked over wooden crates, roses and chrysanthemums in all possible colors. People clicked by in groups of twos and threes, moving with confident, slow walks. I passed face after face. Olive faces, almond eyes, swaths of coal black hair, bone straight and shiny. The most squarish of men slouching and smoking, the most beautiful women clacking over the slick diamond shaped cement tiles in grace-foiling, tropical colored stilettos. Women with high arched brows, flared eyeliner, thick lipstick, dramatic rouge, splashy gold earrings and necklaces. I passed face after face and realized how much I stuck out. With blond hair and blue eyes, with nothing angular or dark about me, nothing strikingly sharp, I made a larger statement than their jewelry, I had no chance of fading into the landscape. I considered purchasing sunglasses to shield part of my round, pale face.

I turned into a quiet neighborhood of apartments. Tin siding, corrugated metal roofs and trellises covered with dense, dusty leaves, strung up lines of laundry, satellite dishes. A woman walked by counting through a wad of U.S dollar bills. I stopped in her path and asked if she spoke English, to ask her where the town center was, but she gave one firm shake of her head and continued walking.

I headed the other direction and came to a bazaar on Buzard Street. The dry, thin air smelled of sweet bread and sour milk. Rows of metal sculptures and paintings of pomegranates and the country's beloved Mount Ararat, packages labeled *Armenian Souvenirs*, full of tiny bottles of *blessed water, soil, and incense*. On card tables, soviet metals lay against dingy, black velvet swatches. A man selling baskets of neatly packaged berries, sectioned by color: white, black, red. Men on benches, paunches out, their eyes straight through me as they played cards, scrunched over small tables, smoking long, thin cigarettes. An older woman walked by selling single roses from a basket, a photograph of a young soldier laminated around her neck.

The street opened up ahead and the town center came into view. What I'd seen on Google images—the Government buildings of Republic Square. Towering buildings in volcanic stone, glistening candy pink in the light of morning. Around a large fountain, a set of boys on rollerblades, children in white and blue school uniforms. Police cars whirled around a traffic circle, honking.

I sat just off the square, under a Coco-Cola umbrella at an outdoor cafe. A sweat drop trickled down from my hairline, stinging my eye, the day's heat beginning to mount. I'd walked further than I'd realized. The dry air was pressing me into a dry, flat version of myself. A kerchiefed woman hunched over a small hay broom, dabbed at the cement around my feet, sweeping cigarette butts into a pile. I got that vague sense of shame that comes with watching the work of others, while sitting and worrying about what you will look like for the rest of the day. A dog passed, mangy and heaving, a vacancy in his eyes, sniffing for scraps. Otherwise the café was empty.

A young server walked my way, showing some hesitation, forcing a smile that she eventually managed to spread over her pretty face as she reached the table. I ordered an Americano and bottle of water.

She wiped some crumbs from the table and into her hand. I shook my head and waved my hand. "Oh I don't mind."

She glanced up, her face saying she'd no idea what it was I'd said but certainly it was unnecessary.

She sprinted off and returned, placing water and coffee in front of me. I tapped the porcelain white coffee cup and asked, "What do you call this in Armenian? This. Armenian?"

Her face resorted to the tenuous, taunt expression she'd began with. "I'm sorry no understand," she said, turning away from my horrible question.

I apologized but she was already far away, busying herself with arranging glasses on a shelf.

The coffee, bitter and gritty, did the job. I ran the mud of it over the roof of my mouth and watched a muted television in the corner. A montage of military training. Images of young soldiers in dark green camouflage, jogging up the side of a brown hill, crouched behind bushes with Kalishnakoffs, laughing around a bonfire, walking single file through a cemetery, their breath visible in the air. It was surprising to see on television in a café, but then I reminded myself it shouldn't be. This was a country that knew genocide, border conflicts past and present, natural disasters. It was far from Alamogordo Airbase but the soldiers wore the same dark green fatigues my father had worn, just before the sand colored camouflage that came soon after, when we took over the Middle East, so I sensed something familiar in the visuals. It brought that ping of sadness that came with reminders of my father.

A shiny black Mercedes SUV pulled up and an immaculate woman climbed out of the back. An hourglass shape, a shimmering white dress, a faint pink hue in her platinum, mermaid hair. I took out my sketchbook and as she passed I tried to catch the way the light fell over her pink mermaid hair. I tried to scribble her down, freeze something of her composition, her fleeting halo, some scrap of her foreign beauty, something to lug with me.

--

Tidy and simple. Paint, sun, building, photograph.

But there's nothing simple about loosening the grip on your life. And nothing tidy about the grip itself. I was fooling myself to think that I was doing something simple for simple reasons. I was fooling myself to think it would be simple to pull off.

Narine knew this but she never tried convincing me not to go any more than she pretended to understand why I would go. Though, she wanted, I think, her words to come along with me for that handful of strange days. She wanted to tell me as much as possible. Even if she knew I was dragging myself in a direction I wasn't quite prepared to go, she was good enough not to deter me from my choice to misstep.

The day I went to Narine's bakery to announce I was going to her home country, she was surprised, too. I didn't tell her my real intentions for going; I never mentioned the framed photo on her wall or wanting to paint that building when the sun moved across it at just the right hour. I just said, "I've decided to go to Armenia."

She laughed and asked, "What do you want to know about it there?"

I had no immediate answer, but she didn't really mind. I shrugged and she shrugged back and said, "Sounds good."

Her reaction made me immediately love her.

## *Yerevan to Gyumri*

Checking out, Hostel Boy asked me why I'd come and where I would go and the only way I could think to say it was "I'm taking a bus to Gyumri to paint pictures."

"To Gyumri to paint pictures," he parroted.

"Yes."

"Gyumri?"

"Yes."

"Why?" His eyes widened, his voice reached a higher pitch before I could answer. "Gyumri! I come from Gyumri! My home. You know the story about Gyumri? You know this? What do you say? The earth moved. You know? Very bad story."

His sudden animation fluttered my stomach. "An earthquake. Yes, I know about it and I'm sorry it happened." I took no time to consider a less generic thing to say, what might feel more right for him to hear.

Hostel Boy said, with something grave on the edge of his voice, "I'm glad you will come to paint pictures in Gyumri. It's a good thing."

I laughed an uncomfortable laugh. I'd shared my reason for being there out loud to someone and out of my head the words sounded strange.

"Thank you," I said.

--

He gave me directions to the bus depot and I left. As I walked over the chipped sidewalk, depleted of much of my morning's energy, I told myself it was a good thing I hadn't shown up carrying more. I considered hailing a taxi and changed my mind, deciding it would only mean more to negotiate—monetarily and otherwise.

As I walked Hostel Boy's words hiccupped through in my head.

*To Gyumri to paint pictures.*

Tidy and simple, I reminded myself.

--

My father had said he'd been around the same age I was when he started drawing, but then the military had won out because he wanted to fly fighter jets, defy gravity, defend his country.

And later in life, I'd gain some clarity about how his flights away from home, at undisclosed places, sometimes for undeterminable amounts of time, had put strain on his relationship to my mother. She'd resented how much he enjoyed his flights away. So maybe Armenia signaled another trait in my blood passed down from him—the desire to flee. But even so, there were more differences than similarities between our two departures. His desires were executed in a professional manner, based on what he deemed as principle and duty. My instance of flight was flimsy, and arguably reactionary. He left a wife and two kids when he took off. I wasn't sure anymore who or what I was leaving.

In Armenia, when I thought of who I'd really left behind, it was a slim list. Frannie, some friends who wouldn't notice my absence for a few days, and perhaps, whether I liked it or not, Eric.

Eric's face rolled loose in my head. And this last memory of him before I left. It was the night I decided to buy the ticket to Armenia, the night I finally told him it was over.

I'd been listening to him rant about red lights. Red lights were the problem with our urban landscape, were the tiny disruptions of every day that ulcerated through him, were the small hiccups contributing to his hypertension. I made the mistake of saying red lights weren't so bad, that I liked the idea of slowing down and enjoying each moment.

"You're spoiling yourself," he said. "All that self-absorbed studying of the world."

I said, "Not true. I like to take time out for myself when it makes sense. I like red lights because they let me go inward, give me time to sit idle. Where's the damage in that?"

He said, "That's why you like to take the long way to my apartment?"

"It's over," I said. "I mean this."

Then I accidentally knocked his beer off my dining room table and it smashed all over the kitchen. He paused, then sighed and let out a loud, throaty "What the fuck! I mean, what the fuck!"

As he yelled he hit his kneecap under the table and I jumped. I wanted to apologize. On any other occasion, that's what I would have done. But instead of talking I stood and watched him roll the broken glass over the heel of his boot.

"You're worse off than I thought," he said. And then, almost in the same breath, "No sorry, it's okay to doubt."

I said, "I don't think this is doubt. To doubt you've got to first know what's in question."

26

I picked up the shards but didn't mop up the beer. The next morning, I felt the stickiness under my feet. Beer settled into the wide grooves of the grain. I left it that way and thought about what I should pack.

--

I reached the queues of vans, each with a paper taped on the passenger window, destinations and departures, rates, information I'd no way of grasping.

"Gyumri?" I said to a man loading crates into the back of one.

"Gyumri," he repeated, nodding.

I managed a window seat on a van jammed full of elderly women and vegetables. As I climbed in, a woman in the front passenger seat turned around and asked if I was French, or so that's how it sounded.

"American," I said with a smile.

She squinted as though stressing her vision to make out my features, then turned back around.

The driver blasted a compilation of robust smooth jazz covers. Lionel Ritchie songs, Stevie Wonder. *I Just Called to Say I Love You* with drum machine and meandering saxophone.

We left Yerevan and hit a moonscape, the narrow road snaking past stones of all kinds. Volcanic pockmarked stones, red stones and mossy stones. Large single stones in the middle of wheat fields, clusters of stones next to jutting trees, next to a dog with a wobbly leg, next to a woman in a long flapping house dress switching a cow on the ass.

The only speed on the highway was an urgent, anxious fast. We weaved like an ambulance and the other drivers weaved right back. Through the front window, a head on collision appeared imminent at all times. I kept to the side window.

We moved toward the mountains, steep ripples of soft pinks and browns. And then beyond, the faint but massive Mt Ararat, its snow top fuzzing out white in the soft blue sky, a giant, frosty smudge on the hot day. I would never have guessed it would be so tall, unreal in its height and it didn't seem natural to see something so snowy in the heat.

I recognized Mt Ararat from most everything I encountered that had to do with Armenia in my reading, internet searching and talks with Narine. In a documentary about the mountain, which I watched long before I'd ever thought to travel near it, they talked about Noah's Ark, the remains of which were believed to be somewhere on the mountain. Through the decades, people ascended the mountain, willing to risk their life to find the ancient shipwreck. Christian explorers, seeking out the tangible evidence of their faith, used the Book of Genesis as their navigational tool. One of them had been an American astronaut in the 70s. John Irwin, the eighth person to walk on the moon. He'd brought moon rocks back to earth. He'd felt God up there on the moon. He'd felt God and came back down to earth a creationist. There were people like him all over the world, all competing to find proof of their faith. Some had been wounded by falling rocks, some got kidnapped by Kurdish rebels, others died from hyperthermia. At one point a climber thought they'd found the ark—an American. But it turned out to be just a natural land formation in the foothills. Upon discovery, though, the Turks, who'd come to claim the mountain as their own through war, sacrificed sheep on the spot in celebration. Later they turned it into a national park. And even after they proved the site was not a shipwreck, the Turks maintained Noah's Ark National Park, and still bus in tourists for picnic lunches today. The documentary said that the astronaut John Irwin had never come down from the mountain with anything newsworthy.

He called it the greatest disappointment of his life. I marveled at that. What it must feel like to devote oneself so much to a cause that failure to secure its evidence would override the success of space travel.

We passed strange tin objects, two worn, black boots sitting aligned on a rock, a man reaping a field, crooked concrete telephone poles, cemented square structures, slouching hay triangles covered with bright blue plastic. We hit a hole in the road disrupting the crates in the back of the van. A stray cantaloupe rolled past my feet.

There was a tapping on my back and I turned to find an old woman lumped together in a blue dress-sack. In her lap she held a glass bowl of sunflower seeds. She scooped seeds into a cone made from a torn square of newspaper and reached out a lumpy arm to hand it to me, her gummy mouth arched up in a smile. I leaned in to hand over a coin I thought was probably right, slightly more than right to be safe, and she pushed my hand away, almost violently, laughing.

--

When Hostel Boy asked if I knew about Gyumri's story, I did. In a way, at least.

I'd tried to learn as much as I could in the time between deciding to go and boarding the plane, either by talking to Narine or skimming the internet. It had been the cultural capital of Armenia, but that ended in 1988 on a cold, December morning. Hostel Boy's story began at 11:41 a.m. that day. That's when the earthquake happened and the hands of his town square's clock froze in place, as though to say *this is where time stops and the story begins.*

This is what I learned of the story. In the seconds that the ground shook, people ran from schools, factories and beds, fish jumped from aquariums, packs of dogs scattered, mattresses fell from their frames, sinks fell through the floor, reinforced concrete collapsed down into sandwiching layers. 20,000 apartments were destroyed, 85% of nine-story buildings were destroyed, 80% of five-story buildings were destroyed, and 25,000 people died. Those still walking sifted debris in search of their families. Shopping bags of relief supplies arrived from Moscow, as did truckloads of equipment, workers from as far as Minsk and blood transfusion equipment and dialysis machines. Dogs from America, trained to seek out survivors buried under rubble. Five tons of clothing arrived from Great Britain. The sun sunk and the sky went dark by half past 5 that afternoon. The survivors lit fires and kept rooting around. They slipped on mud and sunk into holes. They dug and sifted and it began to snow.

According to Narine, some believed the story began because of a Soviet explosion, an underground atomic experiment gone wrong, accidentally detonated bunkers of weaponry. But most assumed the story began because sometimes nature is a cruel force and horrible things happen with little explanation. It's just the shoddy way the earth is put together. Just the natural rupturing of 37 miles of thrust fault, falling between the Alps and the Himalayas, great plates of the earth pushing at each other, smack at the center of the Shirak plateau, 1550 meters above sea level, with the Akhurian river passing to the west, the Pambak mountains to the east and Aragats volcanic range to the south. A seismically active crescent, well inside the collision zone— stretching from eastern Turkey and the Caucasus to the west of the Caspian Sea.

Regardless of why the earthquake happened, it's a fact that the Soviet Union had one uniform building code for an entire territory and so in some ways the story is about the flaws of construction, brick and mortar never meant to hold the people they held for as long as they did.

I think the story must get quiet—that's how I imagine it, anyway. One out of every 12 dead in a town must mute the days. And those left alive, left walking, the souls drained from their heads, sometimes had little to say. But the task of unearthing the living and the dead was loud. Or, so that's how it looks on You-Tube. That's how it reads online. That's how Narine made it seem.

I don't think Hostel Boy was alive yet, but I imagine the earthquake was passed into his blood. Most likely, he came out wailing it at birth.

## *Gyumri*

I found myself standing on the gravel road of the bus lot, the sun going down fast, the dust kicked up. The air was hampered and nothing bustled like in Yerevan. Other than what I intuited, based on the pitch of their voices as two produce vendors argued over who would get the wheeled cart sitting in the road, there was just a flutter of passengers and drivers. I walked to the road and scanned for a queue of taxis but found none. My luggage was getting heavier.

While daydreaming about leaving, I didn't think about how heavy it would be. I hadn't considered how every paint brush I packed would weigh on my body. I'd packed as minimally as I could, though. A small rolling suitcase for clothes and toiletries; an IPad, a portable French easel, a bag of paints, a sketchbook, some pencils and brushes, tucked in a backpack. But still each item took on new weight with every step as I walked a direction I believed would take me to the guesthouse. According to a print out from Google Maps, evidence on paper that I'd thought ahead on behalf of the me who might be lost, it was 1.02 miles to the guesthouse from the bus depot. A straight shot down Tigran Mets Street. With the sun nearly gone in a country of few streetlamps, there loomed a threat of getting lost in new and progressively more terrifying ways.

A dull ache spread from my ribs to my pelvis. I was learning about the strain everyone warned me about after the surgery. I had a history of misunderstanding my body and had taken the illness as a lesson. Since the little man I'd sharpened a focus on my body, a keen awareness of every twinge and every ache. I now regularly took inventory of my body's parts. Arms, muscle, wrist, stomach, back. As I walked I told myself that the dull ache was just indigestion or the onset of monthly cramps. I wasn't sure. With my new keen awareness of all things somatic came a realization that pains manifesting for different reasons could still feel the same. For months I had thought the little man was just the result of not stretching well enough at the gym. Or indigestion. The drawback of my new heightened awareness was that every feeling began to feel like pain.

I brushed away the fear that the trip's exertion might rob me of my recovery. I brushed away the fear that I felt more pain than the average person my age. I brushed away the fear that it would soon be dark. I told myself that what went on in my abdomen, walking in that moment, be it gas or cramps, was a natural part of being alive. I told myself there was no room for doubt or hypochondria. I told myself to focus on getting where I needed to go.

Under my breath I chanted. *Yes, I am curious. Yes, I am not afraid. Yes, I am prepared.* The answers to questions no one had asked.

--

If I would've told anyone I was going, beside Narine, it may have been Frannie—if only out of a bad habit of reluctantly letting her into my world—a world she always seemed right at the edge of, crooking her head for a better look, inquiring, questioning, criticizing.

Frannie would've said not to go, and I had no room for that. I could hear her in my head: *How ridiculous, Sara. Why? You can't afford it.*

She might have listed statistics about disaster risks in earthquake zones, something she'd heard in class or read in some Huffington Post article. And maybe, in a rare display of assertiveness, I'd have told her to shut the fuck up. Or, I would've whined, *But I need to go.* And she'd say, *How could you have healed enough?* And I might have lied, *But I feel great.* And she'd say, *Tell me it doesn't still hurt when you sneeze.* And I'd deny her the satisfaction of being right and tell her *I don't hurt at all.* And she wouldn't believe me. And I'd remind her she told me to be curious, and she'd hate hearing that.

But in the end she'd win because she'd say that I knew what she meant when she said to be curious—camping in Vermont, maybe. Not Armenia.

But she wouldn't *really* win. And neither would I, because we wouldn't be talking about the same thing, we wouldn't even be fighting the same fight.

Frannie always had words of encouragement when I didn't want to be within range of her voice. Her rally cries hit like pebbles flicked at my head. She'd say, *It's what you make of it.* She'd say, *It's just growing pains!* She'd write it down on birthday cards, sign it from her and our mother. *This is going to be the year!*

Once as children, after we'd moved to Maryland, I'd accidently knocked her down when she walked in front of the swing set. She hit a rock and the gash on her forehead left her face a bloody horror. She cried and then I cried. My mother had swooped in, making a rare appearance out of the apartment, and I remember wondering how she could have been on the scene so fast.

Just before sweeping my sister up in her arms, she knelt down to me. "Why would you *do* that?" She said it low voiced, dramatic, shaking, with the sweetness of liquor in her breath.

She did not wait for me to tell her it was an accident. There was no time for my excuses.

Later in the hospital lobby when I saw the butterfly stitches, how they sewed up the part of Frannie I'd torn, I started to cry again. But she was dry eyed by that point. She kicked up her leg and said *You're going to be okay. Don't worry.*

As I walked the quiet Gyumri road, passing still storefronts, sluggish willow trees, stones of all shapes and sizes, my bag slipped from my shoulder, knocking my easel to the ground. I imagined my sister seeing me in that moment.

*Sara, you should have taken only what you could carry.*

I thought about what I'd say to her the next time I saw her. Most likely I'd just apologize for not clueing her in. But maybe I'd pop up at her door and say: *I'm back! See! I knew what I was doing all along.*

That would feel good.

I swallowed the dull nausea that rose up with thoughts of Frannie.

I wondered what she might say back, but in my head I could hardly hear her talking. I'd buried it too far down, the sound of her voice. A small and lovely accomplishment.

--

I'd booked a guesthouse that belonged to Levon. A tall, broad, angular man, casually dressed. Red shiny shorts with matching jersey and blue plastic sandals.

After ringing the bell and announcing who I was, I entered his living room and let my belongings slip from my shoulders onto the elaborate red and gold carpet. I rotated my shoulders and cocked my neck back and forth, relieved to shed the burden.

Levon looked down at my luggage and scratched his chin. He said, "Yes. Okay then."

He bent down and smashed his cigarette into a delicate crystal dish sitting on a white-lace covered table. Other than the low murmur of a TV the house was warm and quiet. It was furnished, tidy and dense with the low hanging smoke from his cigarette. I noted the feminine touches of the room and hoped the matriarch would soon appear. Levon bent down to pick up my luggage. I motioned no, I have it, but he came back with a *no-no-no*, a belly laugh rumbling out of him with a smoker's grumble. He picked up my belongings and I followed him down the hall. I felt acutely how still the house was and began to wonder if we were the only two.

In the guest room, Levon pointed to a neatly folded hand towel sitting on a chair and some mint colored silk slippers, neatly placed at the foot of the bed.

"Yeah?" he asked, maybe more a statement than an actual question, low toned, shrugging his shoulders.

"Yes," I confirmed. "Thank you."

I laughed my anxious laugh. He shuffled back down the hall.

The small room shrank against the weight of a large, elaborately carved wooden chest. A machine gun sat on top of the chest, its tripod mounted to a marble slab. Balancing on the back of the gun sat a fist-sized rock, pocked, chipped and sparkling. The object seemed to say that the room belonged to somebody, maybe someone who'd be back any minute. I found a corner for my luggage and lowered myself onto the hard, twin sized bed like an intruder.

Levon's face appeared in the doorway and I mustered an alert smile to which he responded with a smirk and bowed head. "Please. You come, see books and watermelon."

He motioned me to sit on the couch and disappeared into the kitchen, reappearing with a bowl of melon and a large hardbound book, which he placed on the table in front of me.

"For guests," he said.

He eased into the chair next to me, a chair I could tell was his and his alone, well-worn and shaped to him. Grabbing the remote, he turned the volume up on the television, an interview or news show set to a laugh track.

"Will other guests be joining us?"

When he didn't answer, I concluded we were alone. Or, he just hadn't heard the question. I thumbed through the book— black and white photos of Gyumri.

"There," Levon said, turning in his chair, pointing down to a two-page spread showing a pair of images of the Church of the Holy Savior, dated 1967 and 1988—pre-earthquake and after. The first image, a church. The second image, a cupola resting on the ground. "Churches from earthquake."

I said, "It's amazing that could happen. I've heard about this church and how it's yet to be rebuilt. Still sitting in pieces in the town's square."

He'd already turned back to the television. "I do not understand," he mumbled.

I realized he meant he didn't understand me.

--

A skeleton key in the guest room door offered the option to lock myself in and I did. Lying on top of the bed, not bothering to find my way under the blankets or even to change my clothes, a dull panic rolled through my already achy muscles. I turned to my side and the gun with the rock on it stared down at me. The wind jerked the bedroom door in its frame and though I knew what it was, I imbued it with significance, a foreshadowing of things to come.

I got up to dig out my iPad, deciding it time for a more familiar world, for sending messages home. But there was no Wi-Fi signal, though the guesthouse's website listed it as an amenity. Not even a prompt for a password. Levon's Guesthouse website was a fraud and now I was sure he was, too. Levon could be anyone. Lying under the gun I told myself he was nobody to fear. That it was only a few days. That it was okay that I'd come without telling anyone. That soon enough everyone would get the emails I owed them.

--

I went back to the bakery a few days after telling Narine I was going to Gyumri. She sat one table over, folding plastic ware into white napkins, eyes on the task as she talked. The bakery was otherwise empty.

I didn't bring it up but she said, "I'm delighted you'll go, but it confuses me. I have people for you to contact, I'll give you numbers. They could help you, but they don't speak English, so…" She drifted off with a shrug of her shoulders.

"It's okay," I said.

The young man normally stationed in the kitchen came out to empty the trash bins and the tenuous expression he flashed me said they'd be closing. After he shuffled back to the kitchen I asked Narine if he was her son and she paused her hands. "I don't have kids," she said. What I took to be annoyance ran thick through her words.

I felt like I should apologize for asking, but decided instead just to leave without ceremony. As I placed my cup in the bin above the trashcan, Narine raised her head and put down the plastic ware.

"Gyumri will be a mystery to you."

Her grave expression broke and she gave me an unchar-acteristically broad smile, broader than usual, before lowering her head back to her task. She shook her head with animation, as though to say no, or that she wouldn't get through to me, or that she'd just witnessed something indecent, but more funny than embarrassing.

As I pushed the door to leave, Narine called out, "What-ever it is you want to affirm or reaffirm. Whatever it is, you may find it there. But likely you won't. You will find many other things you didn't expect. "

All I could think to say was, "Thank you."

# 3

I woke to a small gray bird jabbering on the windowsill and realized I must have fallen asleep after all. Scooping myself up, I smoothed my hair, put jeans on and emerged from the guest bedroom into the hard light of the house.

Levon stood in the kitchen over a pan of frying eggs.

"Melik," he said, pointing to a gangly twenty-something sitting at the table, tapping the side of his coffee cup and tentatively smiling from under a floppy black hat. He looked tired. They both did. I must have, too.

Levon handed me a cup of coffee and motioned me to sit at the table across from Melik. I hoped he was a guest or family but Melik introduced himself as a neighbor brought over to translate what I might have to say this morning.

"Levon's English is not so great," he said flatly, still tapping the side of his cup.

The night before, I'd pointed to the pictures in Levon's book making comments about each one, just to ease the awkwardness, to have something to do with myself as Levon and I sat side by side. It didn't matter so much what came out of my mouth, or whether he could understand me. What mattered was the guise of an exchange. Me talking, and him nodding and grunting intermittently, jerking his large head back and forth from television to book. A sufficient enough means of moving the night along. I'd assumed Levon had agreed.

Melik ran his finger around the bottom of his cup, swirling the stray grounds. Levon wants to understand why you are here. He has questions."

"Questions? I mostly just want to paint."

"But what will you paint? I mean, Levon knows this but he wants to know what you want to paint."

I asked Melik why it mattered, my skin warming, my pulse thickening. I reminded myself to stay level, buried my face in the coffee cup, I thought of Narine, her Armenian coffee and the delicate cups she served it in. Not so different than Levon's cups—flower patterned, narrow and fragile. I'd thought the same thing the night before, staring down at the woven rug in Levon's living room. The most quotidian objects reminded me of her and suddenly I almost missed her. Or, maybe I missed the familiar setting of her bakery. Or, of being familiar myself.

Levon kept his face to the stove, flipping eggs around the pan.

"He wants to help," Melik said. "To make sure you are okay. He's worried. He doesn't understand why you would come here."

I did the defensive laugh. "He shouldn't be worried. It's fine."

Melik, flat-toned and calm, pressed on with his perfect English, "But he is and he will be. No it's good. But how, I mean, Levon would like to understand *how* he can help make your stay better."

I forced a breeziness through my words. "Oh, no need. I know it will be fine."

I dismissed the cramp in my chest and an impulse to scurry back to my room, figuring such a move would cause more harm than good, or at least more attention. I ran my index fingers under my eyes and scanned the tips for clumps of mascara.

Levon finally lifted his head from the stove, said something to Melik in Armenian, flailing an arm in the air. He was dressed for work, stiff slacks and a button down shirt, his thin silver strands of hair slicked away from his broad forehead. In his native language, his words had more strength and his body moved lighter. He was a different person altogether, he was himself again, no doubt thankful for not having to put energy into being someone else for my sake. For that morning at least, he could give up trying to understand me, relinquish control of the moment, revert just a little bit back to his own life.

Levon leaned over from the stove, shoved a plate of eggs, breads and cheeses toward me.

"You," he grumbled.

I thanked him and smashed a slab of cheese on a thick wedge of bread. Breakfast wasn't included on the amenities list when I booked the room. I silently told myself I'd have to confirm my rate, not having yet paid, soon but at a later point. For the moment I didn't want to engage, I just wanted an escape from the kitchen, from the whole house.

So, it surprised me when, maybe as a means of talking to make the moment less awkward, I started explaining to Melik and Levon, both sitting across from me, silently eating eggs, why I was there. How back home in a bakery, there was a photo of an old Soviet era structure that apparently sat at the southernmost edge of town. A white concrete shell of a building, just sitting like an ancient ruin. "I'm going to go paint it," I said.

Melik paused his chewing, "Yes, of course. I know the place."

"Yeah?"

"We call it Ghost Town. I can take you."

I considered this, immediately recognizing that it made better sense than setting out on my own. I had no exact address. Somehow I hadn't thought that part out.

"Well okay, sounds good." I said, intending to sound matter-of-fact.

I slipped my cup and plate in the sink and skulked to the bathroom, scouring out some cleaner version of myself in lukewarm water, unable to figure out the hot water heater. I caught the sag of my eyes in the mirror, two ruddy bags, and said *so be it*.

--

Melik offered to carry my supplies and easel but I wouldn't have it and to say as much I slung everything over my shoulders with enough force that he let out a breathy laugh, acknowledging the melodrama of my motions, before pivoting on his heels and adjusting his hat down into his eyes. We descended the stairs to the yard and the previous day's pain from rib to abdomen began nudging to my surface. I sensed the heat of a blister at my heel ready to erupt and pleaded with my body to stop all the fuss. And though I wondered how far we'd walk, I knew I couldn't, wouldn't ever ask.

The neighborhood was an eerie quiet, like the sound, too, was washed out under the sun. I craved the sunglasses I didn't bother getting in Yerevan. The dust hung visible, swelled my nose and caked the roof of my mouth.

Melik said, as though I'd asked, "No, I don't live here anymore. I'm only visiting, back from France where I live with my French wife. But I was raised here. Here." He stopped to point at a bottom floor apartment with windows lined in an intricate metal lattice. A small, potted plant with a lone pomegranate struggling to take shape and redden sat by the door.

"I can't live here anymore," he said. "But, anyway, I should explain Levon. Usually it's Armenians or Russians because Russian is his other language, or even some diasporans, a few Germans who speak some Russian, but you are the first American so this is new for him." He walked slightly ahead of me, flashing half glances my way. "It's just not what he is used to."

On the main road, we walked by a white trailer on wheels, rusting orange and a jutting up slice of corrugated tin, curled and propped against a clutter of rocks, more rock structures, cluttered up next to other rock structures.

I asked Melik what Levon did for work because it seemed like an easy, necessary question, a logical direction to steer the topic of Levon, and he told me he was a bank manager who spent his days granting and denying money to others.

"Levon is considered a good, popular man in town," he said with a sudden lift to his words that told me he was proud of his neighbor.

I asked if anyone lived with Levon, another necessary question, and learned his daughter, son and wife had moved to Yerevan. I didn't ask any more after that, but I didn't need to because Melik slowed his pace some, lowered his voice and continued, "See, the neighbors are catching on to the fact that he's been renting out his house to guests. It makes no sense that so many strange faces would come and go around the neighborhood. Some have asked Levon about his guests and he's been open about it but feels it's none of their business. And it's true it's none of their business. It's not his duty to justify himself to anyone, though he'd prefer if colleagues at the bank didn't know about this because they'd tease him for needing money and looking desperate but that is shitty too. He probably won't do it forever, and he hasn't been doing it for more than a few months, but for now, he's opening his house to guests to raise money to send his son to the London School of Economics. And also because the house is too large for one person."

I said, "It's funny. I thought when I booked my stay online it was a room in a guest house, not a home stay."

"No it's a guest house," Melik replied flatly.

I thought to push it, to learn more about Levon, but didn't. Instead I tried conjuring something new to say, but could sense only dissonance bubbling in me, some off key something I'd regret pulling up and out of my mouth. I didn't want to look too invested in knowing. I'd arrived with another purpose. So I focused on the goal of moving forward, the goal of seeing what would come from some paint on a canvas I'd carried thousands of miles. I let a childish disdain for Melik's presence come over me, to feel the irritation of walking with someone I'd made no room for on my agenda. I hadn't thought out how difficult it might be to find the building in the photograph, but I'd envisioned myself arriving alone. I doubted Melik knew I was irritated, that I found walking with him to be a laborious task, but it's possible he knew because he stopped talking. He let me go on in silence. And I appreciated that about him.

At an empty building with a sign taped over a cracked window, Melik stopped and translated. "That is for rent." He took out his cell phone, typed in the number on the sign and shrugged. "Maybe to open a pub." He laughed under his breath.

We walked on and the road began to widen. Twenty minutes of walking and we'd reached the industrial outskirts. A vacant factory complex, rusted cranes, worn Russian letters on a metal fence, an abandon gas station, five stories of a building smooshed half to the road.

"That was Shirak hotel," said Melik, watching me look at the building. "Earthquake. But most buildings like this are now occupied."

I feared sounding overly dramatic or not dramatic enough, so I just shook my head and sighed, resigned to staying silent, my reactions buttoned up so they couldn't be wrong.

We cut through a field, in the distance a shanty town made of rusted shipping containers with stones and boulders to hold the tin roofs in place clustered like a rash. A small church made of a red stone sat nearby.

"The church was built by someone rich now living in Russia," Melik explained. "But the rest of it, we call these *domiks*, these houses. *Domiks* means tiny houses in Russia. Like disaster houses. Where they put people waiting for housing after the earthquake. Twenty-five fucking years and counting. And that running along is Shit River. The *domik* toilet. Wild marijuana once grew here." He giggled.

A boy darted over, skipping along sideways, the first person to pass on our walk, tinged brown, his hair and clothes, smudged with the dust of the town. He shouted something and Melik translated that he wanted to know why he'd walk a woman through this neighborhood.

The boy stopped in his tracks, laughing.

Melik translated again. "He says 'What do you want to show? What could you possibly want to see? We have a very dirty neighborhood!'"

I sensed it was nearing noon, the hour of strongest light, the best light for painting. I asked if we were close and Melik nodded yes. The smudged boy continued along with us at a distance.

--

The noon light glittered and the shadows gripped the field of Ghost Town. There were colors I never would have known from Narine's picture. The yellow of buttercups, the purple of chicory, the whites and ochres of snarled weeds, the occasional red dots of rose hips, the blue and orange of the gravel. It was anything but drab. And the buildings themselves. Not just one, but several. Like a line of slouching silver top hats stacked far off on the horizon. Each structure with its own holes and missing parts through which the light darted in and out. Each torn apart in its own way. I couldn't figure out which building I'd shown up to see.

Squinting toward the limpid white sky, I said to Melik, "The light here. How to explain it?"

Melik, cross-legged on the ground, fingering a blue rock, explained—as though answering the question he'd expected me to ask—just what the buildings had been. "For Soviet soldiers. Only half built when the earthquake happened and that was it. They just left the buildings behind unfinished and forgotten. People are breaking apart the buildings to sell in chunks or to work on their *domik* homes, sometimes dying by climbing into the building and trying to take it apart."

I wanted to know more but stopped short and walked deeper into the field. I thought I heard Melik say something else, but if he did it was inaudible through the hard wind and I let it go. The site of my sutures itched in the heat and I resisted the urge to lift my shirt and scratch. I chose a location and dropped my supplies, putting the buildings at roughly the same distance as the one in the picture. A parched sound came from under the weight of all that I'd dragged with me, some clicking bugs, some crickets in the weeds.

My sister was right with her impression of the photo. The bright field was reminiscent of Alamogordo. That sky, that vastness. I tried to imagine an f-15 flying overhead, which was how I always recalled the skies of Alamogordo, but anything of such force, such human-made speed and sound, seemed impossible in a place like this.

And then it struck me, for the first of many times while I'd be there, that I really had no idea what I was doing. My simple task of painting a building was now not as simple as I'd promised myself, and the new complications made my head throb. I had no idea where to begin. The heat had a force to it. The colors were nothing like I'd thought they'd be. In the last three days I'd slept very little. A blister throbbed on my heel. I'd had to rely on others to find this location and the location was full of far more buildings than I would have known.

I turned around to find Melik walking my direction.

"You don't have to stay," I yelled.

"Of course I will stay."

"Please. No."

Maybe I sounded aggressive or anxious. He responded only by lifting his hands in comical defense. "I will come back for you."

"It won't be necessary."

"But just in case."

"Just in case what?"

"I will feel guilty if I don't walk you back. And Levon will be angry with me. When the sunsets there are wild dogs. You never know." He shrugged his shoulders.

On the road yards away a car passed and a sloshing noise cut through the sound of the field, reminding me the human world lived not so far off. I considered my visibility to people driving by and couldn't determine if it spooked or comforted me.

I said to Melik, "Give me four hours."

He tipped his hat, turned on his heels and walked toward the road.

It settled in that there were people within walking distance who felt accountable for me, even though I hadn't asked for it. There were people who wanted to warn me about wild dogs. People who wanted to make sure I got where I needed to go.

I turned to my task, pulled my hair back and stretched out the legs of my easel.

Melik's voice came through the wind again. I turned to find him jogging back toward me. "Sometimes you may hear hammers. Banging." He made a fist and mimed banging a hammer. "It only means they are taking the buildings apart.

Don't worry. They will be friendly if they see you. But I would not go inside the buildings. Sometimes they crumble."

"No problem."

He waved, turned and jogged away, holding his hand over his head to keep his hat in place. I watched until he disappeared up the road, until I was sure he was gone.

--

In the field of Ghost Town, I lined up tubes, bottles and brushes next to my easel. I'd realized while packing that I wouldn't be working big there. No broad stretched canvases. The paint had to dry fast, so only acrylic would work. Preferring to work big and with oils, the alternate sizes and materials suddenly seemed like a hindrance to accomplishing what I'd set out to do, and I wondered how I was going to make it work.

I looked at my watch and realized I'd spent nearly half an hour laying out supplies in a logical order. I was stalling, relishing the one task where my control began and ended. Everything else was left to chance. The color, light, the buildings on the horizon, I needed to unlock a starting point, a shape, but I had no clue where to start. I'd come following light. It was the light in the photo that caught me. But that sounded almost weightless out there where it was real, where it blinded and dehydrated me. So I sat on the field, staring at the horizon line, a straightforward structure, with the limited range of tones, and took in the unblinking light until my eyes stung and watered.

As I studied the changing light of that dead center hour, shadows grew defined and rooted to the objects they attached themselves to. One of the few times Eric critiqued my work, he had called it 'fetishized studies of light.' He'd called it 'cold.' He said he meant it as a compliment, but I didn't see it and eventually would conclude he just didn't know how to talk about art.

The light that beat down on my subject and my shoulders was not cold, and I was not cold in it. Of that much I was confident.

The light was anything but white but white was what I preferred to build from. Eventually I started with a primer of it, moving on to dabbing in ochre and the slightest blacks and reds. The paint dried fast in the heat. After an hour, all I'd gotten down was somersaulting color, but it was a beginning. I took it as achievement.

And the greatest part, the true signal of something accomplished: For that hour I hadn't thought of home. I hadn't thought of my stupid job or the people who would have objected to me going to Gyumri.

I lay down on my back, closed my eyes and listened for the sound of hammers. Only wind filled my ears and the clicking of weeds and bugs. A fly came by. My heart sounded in my throat and my breathing hovered in my neck. The sun tingled pink over my eyelids and stung my skin. Sweat evaporated, leaving a bleachy smell in my nostrils. I'd never known such brightness and heat. I needed water but had only brought enough for my brushes.

I got up for a better look at the buildings and wondered why I hadn't gone close to begin with, why I'd chosen to keep them on the horizon, in similar scale as Narine's picture. And in approaching them, the buildings changed. Rubble building in the corners rendered the structures knobbed rather than pointed, less square than jagged, their incompleteness became more apparent.

I bent my head and climbed through the open gash of a would-be window. I entered the guts of it. It was dank and almost cool. A scattering of plastic bags skirted the floor. I tripped on a loose piece of gravel and recovered, sneezing dust and debris. In the distance, on the other side of the field, beyond the horizon line I'd stared at for hours, an abandoned car frame sat upside down. And beyond that, some kind of complex under construction with what looked like solar panels on its roof.

A sadness hit. Sadness for how easy it would be to have called it all nothing. Or to call it broken. Or, empty. Just abandoned arrangements of blocks, rust and stone, left in mid-fall, slowly getting chipped away.

On the ground, in the dirt between the wide cracks of concrete, what I thought could be animal prints spanned the length of the building's frame. *A bear? Wolves? The wild dogs.* I wondered what to do if a wild dog pack came.

*Was it waving your arms? Keeping still?*

Something about the inside of the building reminded me how no one knew where I was. No one other than Levon and Melik. At first it washed over me as a sort of freedom, or an almost freedom, a strange kind of welcomed loneliness. But then I considered what might happen if I twisted an ankle or broke a leg walking over all that debris and rock or while running from a wild animal.

There was the inherent problem attached to the freedom of aloneness: there will be no one to assist if you can't assist yourself. The problem felt familiar—the problem of being alone—and the problem felt good.

I couldn't get away from the worry of breaking my body, but was in a good enough mood to accept it as an instinctual, necessary thinking. Survival thinking.

I decided the best thing to do was just sit.

--

Things were never perfect but it hadn't been all bad, those months with Eric. It started with promise but it eventually got hard to recollect what the good was, to extract it from the ugly.

We met in a bar, the exact place I always said I refused to meet men. At the bar he ordered us gin and tonics, making a show of calling the bartender by name. He pronounced himself a filmmaker.

When I mentioned I painted he said, "You're an artist, too. Yes, of course you are."

"Do I look like an artist?" I asked. It wasn't a particularly artsy bar.

"You do. It's in your eyes." He fanned his hands over my face in the way a magician might over a hat containing a soon-to-be pulled out rabbit. I learned fast how prone to exaggerated motions he was. Motions equal parts ironic comedy and a plea for attention.

It became clear fast in that first conversation that we were not in the same places with our crafts. As artist we'd little in common. He'd managed to establish a media firm by age 25, and lamented that these days he spent too much time appeasing the CEOs of start-up firms and retails chains and not enough time seeing the films in his head come to fruition. He admired the route I'd chosen.

"You've stayed true to the work," he said, rubbing a hand over his thick, product-heavy waves. Even his hair beckoned the attention of onlookers.

I scoffed at the idea. *The work.* To think that I was on any sort of trajectory. My timidity embittered me. I'd gone to art school and came out the other side on a rickety path to no specific future. I kept painting, yes, but I hadn't solidified good relationships with the right people. I hadn't the confidence to push my work forward. I hadn't a stomach for rejection.

"Why are you rolling your eyes," he asked.

I told him I'd decided against New York, where the idea of living in a 250 square foot apartment didn't seem worth the career advancement that might come with it. It was a half-truth at best. New York had never even seemed in the cards.

"Well, it's just getting you in the right places, in front of the right people. You don't need to live in New York to have a presence there. I know people. I might be able to help."

I perked up, stopped rolling my eyes and let him order more gin and tonics.

I should have been weary that all this got relayed over the course of an initial conversation in a bar, while getting increasingly drunk. But I chose to leave that night thinking some development lurked not far off. Maybe this was meant to be and not just wishful thinking. I woke the next day, head pounding, and still clung to most of those wishful thoughts.

And so within three weeks we were on a train to New York. We stayed in Brooklyn with his sister, a demur and shy graphic designer who shared his button nose and wavy locks. I learned fast that this was the connection he was referring to. And I learned fast, sitting around the half-packed cardboard boxes in her studio apartment's living room, in between her crying jags and bathroom trips, that she was in the midst of a divorce.

For much of the day I found myself walking the streets of Dumbo, Brooklyn, letting the siblings have their space. They'd put up no resistance when I offered to do as much.

Later that night we went to an opening in Chelsea, an opening that may or may not have been a friend of Eric's sister. For most of the hour we spent there, his sister sat on a leather couch near the bathroom, snuggled and hugged by various passersby. I focused on seeking new ways of staring at the art on the walls—framed collages of torn up twenty-dollar bills. Eric worked the room.

He'd indicated his sister would be the one with all the friends at the opening, not him, but it was him winning the room, pouring himself plastic cup after plastic cup of wine and telling what from a distance looked like complicated jokes with spot-on punchlines. In three weeks I'd noticed he could be magnetic and hysterical—traits that he could manipulate easily, turning the knobs higher or lower—depending on how much the room needed working.

Then he did that thing he would do time and time again when I was ready to throw in the towel. When I was convinced that the dead end had presented itself, he'd do something to make it all better.

I walked over to Eric, nudged his side and he stopped talking, changed course and said, as though I'd just walked into the room, "Here she is, ladies and gentlemen, this woman here, this beautiful artist from Washington D.C., she is as talented a painter as she is beautiful."

I gave a shy wave to the crowd of four or five and received nods, some limp shaking of some hands. I turned and poured a full cup of wine. The crowd dispersed quickly after my introduction.

In the moment it didn't bother me so much. Eric had called me beautiful, talented. He had halted his momentum, turned the knob down to proclaim his interest in me, to proclaim I was worthy of conversation. And I let that matter most. It just wasn't my crowd or my town. If that could have been my invitation to better understand New York's gallery world—and who could say that it was—I hadn't grabbed it.

But gradually it sank in. I would come back to that moment time and again. That introduction to a handful of Chelsea gallery goers became a symbol for my failure to embrace artistic ambition. It became the chance that slipped past. The conversations I didn't have. The conversations I would go on to have in the mirror when stalling before work. I'd mouth my clever replies to imaginary questions to myself while putting on makeup. Alone I mastered all the ways in which I could have been some better, alternate me: *Hello, I'm an artist from D.C. and I'm here to tear things wide open. I am here to eat it alive. This man who brought me here, I do not need him to be here. I have not known him long enough for him to take my whole, racing heart—this jittering heart I want to hand over to you now. I'm ready to talk to you about how things might just fall into place after all.*

Eric never mentioned that I'd botched my chance that night. At first I thought it was to spare me the embarrassment, but later it seemed that the event just hadn't registered for him, and for the rest of our relationship he never said anything about that night or that trip, other than to give updates on his sister's divorce.

On the way back from New York I'd asked, "You did know about your sister's break-up, right?"

"Can you believe her husband hates for her to wear sunglasses? Says that it's bourgeois. She'll be better without him."

It was like that sometimes. I had a question and he had the answer to what he wanted to discuss.

--

I heard Melik's voice and stood to wave out a hole where a door might go. From the opposite end of the field, he yelled that I shouldn't be in there and I yelled back that it was fine. I wanted to believe it was fine. And as he ran toward me, I wanted to say I didn't want anyone running to me with a message that said otherwise, because that shouldn't be too much to ask. But all I did was backtrack in silence, watching my every step.

--

Gyumri's Vartanants Square, the town center, was edged with sinewy evergreens wearing the old, dusty scraps of Christmas decorations. Dingy, dull red ribbons and sparse strands of blue electric icicles. Melik took me to the only restaurant on the square, a Russian place he described as "a business too large for a town of people who can't afford the luxury of dining out." In the sleepy-amber lit interior, its walls lined in the fur of large bears and woven rugs, long-faced men sat around large wooden tables, drank beer, their legs tightly crossed. Melik and I sat at an umbrella table out front. We scooped chunks of beef from bowls of deep red borsch and picked from a mountain of warm bread.

What few people walked by on Vartanants Square glanced back as they passed me, confusion clear on their faces, a confirmation I'd disrupted order with my presence. I added a smudge to an otherwise predicable landscape. People didn't clip by cool and confident like they did in Yerevan. In Gyumri they dragged a little. Their old Russian sedans clunked by slow and squeaky. Gyumri had fewer high heels, less make-up, more weathered and leathery faces.

Several women looked like versions of Narine. Women with thick dark waves of hair falling along thin faces. Maybe I was seeing Narine's sisters and aunts and cousins.

There'd been a day not long before I left when Narine had handed me my bag of tabbouleh along with a folded piece of paper—phone numbers and names, written out in blue curling cursive, paper pulled from a spiral notebook. "Just in case," she shrugged, pressing my hand between hers and squeezing. "They are people I know."

I wondered if any of the women passing weren't some of the people she knew.

A movie screen standing in the center of the square was lit up with the large, glowing head of Cher. Her shiny made up face, her voice filling the violet evening air, and I laughed at the suddenness of a Cher looming over a mostly empty town center.

Melik lifted his eyes from his bowl and explained with his thin apathetic tone that Cher is actually Armenian. I stopped laughing, embarrassed, but then Melik laughed, too, which made me laugh even harder. I laughed a laugh that loosened me. The headache that had mounted from hours of dehydration was subsiding and the pending blister on my foot and the stiff in my shoulders had eased to a tolerable level.

I felt like talking, so I asked Melik why he came back from France. He said that three years ago he'd married a French volunteer and when he did he promised himself he'd never come back to Armenia. But there he was. He figured he'd be back in France soon, but couldn't say when.

He leaned in and lowered his voice as though divulging a secret, "The short answer, the easy answer, as to what brought me back, is I wanted to see family. But the most accurate answer to your question. I'm a writer in need of some space to work. Space to be a writer, but mostly just for the space to be. I'm working on a story that traces a man's walk down a mountain, back home to his village. In the story not much happens. It's more meditative. A character tries to find something he thinks was ripped apart from him and diluted. He knows only that it is at the bottom of the hill, but he has no idea what he is looking for. He knows only that he is not complete without it and he's hungry to complete himself. But as the journey down the hill continues he grows more upset. More frustrated and confused. The mountain's too foggy to see anything and the man must find his way down. He scrapes himself on trees and rocks and at one point lies down and takes a nap. The story goes in and out of dream. The main character meets many people along the way. Really, it's just a reflection of how I feel in France. Alienated and floating. It's funny being back here in Gyumri because it feels like home and I can get a lot of work done and be focused but then sometimes I just lay down and take a nap because the town is so sleepy. I sleep a lot here but work well, too. In France I wake up many times through the night. I get too distracted to write. Plus, here I can earn money from my family's business making gravestones. I suppose I could not return to France, and take over the family business. It's one option. But who knows? Now let's talk about you. Why'd you come?" Melik nodded his beer toward me before taking a long swallow.

Caught off guard by the shift to me, I explained I'd been sick and had surgery and the idea came while my body was healing. Melik placed his soup bowl down and blinked in a way I took to mean he wanted further explanation. I worked to finesse my thoughts into something and offered some simple explanation of the tumor—what it was and how it made itself known to me. He didn't speak, only nodded, rubbed his temple with his glass, and cast his eyes far away. His silence, his distance, and my own beer kept me babbling.

"So when it was clear it wasn't going to kill me, that I wasn't dying, after the surgery I decided I needed to understand my body and my mind within a new framework. I needed to push against my limits, to see that they were not limits at all. I mean I was healed but still mentally not right. I needed to experience myself somewhere new. My sister urged me to be more curious. That curiosity about the world would get me out of my head and into the world. My head would naturally adjust. My sister is always like: *you make lemons out of lemons, never lemonade.* It's one of her sayings. She's studying to be a social worker. I decided to take her advice. I'm on a medical leave of absence from my job because of the surgery and since it's far longer than I needed to recover I thought, *why not.* So, now I'm here. I can barely afford it even for just a few days but it felt like it needed to happen."

Melik pinched his eyes together in a way that confirmed how sloppy I sounded. "None of that really explains why you would come *here*, why would your sister tell you to come here?" He smirked. "You came to paint. She felt like you needed to come here and paint. Specifically, here?"

"No she didn't tell me to come here." I shrugged, "It's complicated."

"Because of a photo of Ghost Town," he said, matter-of-factly.

"Yes. I mean, I knew it when I asked the owner of the photo to explain what the photo was. You could call the picture a sort of catalyst. I'd been looking at that image in the bakery down the street from my house for years and the curiosity about it had just become a kind of white noise in my head. Then finally it clicked. I realized that there was no reason not to ask about the photo. And so I asked my question and got my answer. But, and I can't really describe this part, it didn't make sense to just ask and know about the photo's context. It just felt like something else had to happen. The image suddenly had context, sure, but I was overcome with some longing to understand the context—an urge to connect some sort of action to my new understanding of the image. So, I thought to myself, why not come and see and record the image for myself. Really, it's simple when you think about it."

"So you are here to create some sort of record?"

"Something like that I guess."

"And what will you do with the record, your painting, when you get back?"

"I can't say I've thought that far ahead."

"There was a time in history, maybe Italy, where the artist was encouraged to watch torture. To see the facial expressions of the wounded and killed. To see just what blood looks like."

"I've heard that. Caravaggio."

"What do you do back in America?"

"Caravaggio was known for tenebrism. They said his contrast of light and shadow was violent."

"What is your work? Profession, I mean."

I hadn't fooled him into thinking I was an artist for a living. "I sit a lot," I said. "Stare at a computer screen and try to look busy."

"I still don't get it, why you chose here. But it's not my business."

Melik went quiet again, his eyes returning to that faraway place. He was done interrogating me.

In our silence I retreated into assumptions about how Melik must have seen me. Not what his impressions of me were as a person, but rather what he thought of my appearance. I'd reached a heavy buzz from the beer and my stomach bloated. I declared to myself that he himself was attractive but the shape of his face looked elongated from the profile, especially in his hat, and so he was most attractive face on. I'd sweated through my shirt at the pits and imagined I was at my worst. I wished I knew what his wife looked like and considered asking more about her, but it didn't feel like the time. I cocked my head and let it rest on my knuckles to keep it in a firm place.

It was nearly dark and the air had cooled. The square, full of taxis parked diagonally along the road, seemed more awake. More of the town wandered across the square, or sat on the lip of the trickling marble fountain in the middle of the square. Cher was replaced by some piped in marching band sound, something dramatic and oddly loud with an austere, Soviet vibe.

I needed to break the silence that threatened to make all the ease I had gained vanish from me.

"I hate my work, actually."

"You do?"

"Crawl spaces."

"Crawl spaces?" He leaned in as though I was about to divulge incredible secrets.

"Yeah, house crawl spaces. The company I work for remodels crawl spaces. I work in the office. Me and two other women. I convince myself every day that it's okay not to feel passion about my job. It had started out as a temp job but then I just stayed. But it allows me the headspace to make artwork. To live out the real life I was meant to live. Though most days, honestly, that life couldn't feel further away. And I know too much about crawl space science. They called it that. Crawl space science. I know about all things basement and less and less about what it means to be hungry to make my artwork work. You know in some way it was a sweet relief to pass out from pain that day in the office when the tumor ruptured. To be swept away and then later granted flowers and cards, quick emails and texts to get well soon and a few weeks off."

Melik nodded and gave me an empathetic smile. It was clear he had no idea what to do with me. I swallowed back my instinct to apologize for the rant. We finished our beers almost simultaneously and I was drunk.

"Okay, follow me," Melik said.

We walked in silence, a block past the square, just past the music and lights of the town center, to the Church of the Holy Savior—the church in Levon's book. The semi-ruined building was meshed in scaffolding, the cupola rested next to it on the ground. Other than the scaffold it looked exactly like the picture.

"It's finally starting to look like a church again, don't you think?" Melik raised his arms and chuckled.

I asked, the question coming out unexpectedly, "Do you think it's impossible for me to understand this place? To understand a thing like this, for example. A church in permanent reconstruction?"

"What is the nature of understanding? I mean, impossible is such a big word. What is mysterious about a broken church and who am I to say if you can or cannot understand it?"

--

The day I'd knocked Eric's beer onto my floor, that day we fought about red lights and I finally decided to say it was over, we'd been at his daughter's birthday party. It was also the day I learned he had a daughter. He'd conceived her eight years earlier with an acupuncturist who lived on a farm, thirty-some miles outside the city. As a couple they hadn't lasted long enough for him to be invited to the hospital when the acupuncturist went into labor. He'd been granted no stake in naming the child.

"Rose," Eric spit out as he drove. "*Rose*. What kind of name is that?"

When we got in his truck that day I'd thought we were headed out for an afternoon drive in the country, as advertised. I'd welcomed it, too, having recently had some shaggy black pit of me drudged up and dropped onto a cool steel plate, the pain still spiking in my shoulders and smarting at my gut. It seemed a good way to ease back into the world. But I was to be the arm candy who arrived next to Eric on Rose's doorstep, on the farm, thirty-some miles outside of the city, the one who'd prove to the acupuncturist mother that Eric was a stable enough man to have a girlfriend.

We were only minutes from Rose's house when Eric told me she existed, close enough that I had no real time to protest and the car was going too fast to jump out.

"No way," I said.

"It doesn't have to be the end of the world," he said. "I bought her a piñata. I signed the card from us both."

I went along with it. Upon introduction, I leaned down to Rose and looked in her glassy blue eyes, and I told Rose *Happy Birthday.* Cheerily. As though it was what I wanted to be doing, as though I wasn't embarrassed at all.

An hour later, in the truck, driving those thirty some miles back to the city, Eric said, that when he met me, he thought, *This one, she'll stick around. She's not going to go anywhere.*

He said, "I introduced you because I have confidence in you. I kept it from you because I wanted the time to be just right."

"Confidence that I won't go anywhere?"

"Confidence you won't go anywhere."

"Because I'd have nowhere else to go?"

"Don't be so melodramatic."

"I can't have kids."

"Yeah."

"It's true they told me after the surgery."

"Well—"

"It's okay."

"Yes, it will be okay. I mean, actually I knew."

"You knew?"

"Your sister."

"Oh please no."

"Don't worry."

"I'm not worried. I mean I don't really even like kids."

It was the first time I'd said it out loud. It didn't sound so bad, and it felt pretty good. Like laying down a heavy weight. And the look on Eric's face, that look of disapproval nearing disgust, drove the good feeling home. I had won a round for once.

--

Inside Levon's house, inside the small room where I slept, standing on the bed to get a better look at the stone balancing on the back of the machine gun on top of the cabinet, I rubbed my hand over the rock and accidently dislodged it from its glued spot. The rock fit easily in my hand. I tried replacing it in a half-moon wedge of dried glue, but couldn't force it back into place.

I placed the rock next to the gun and carefully moved away, my pulse thick in my throat. For the remaining night hours, I lay stiff under thin sheets, feeling the weight of the dark, a dull ache in my chest, knowing I'd done the wrong thing, touched the wrong object. I'd changed the room, I'd undone something. How easy it is to fuck up a scene.

I whispered, *Tomorrow I will buy some glue and put the rock back in place and everything will be okay.*

*How dare I?*

I whispered to myself and the house creaked with Levon, his cigarette smoke seeping through the door cracks along with the living room's yellow light. Evidences of a man who never slept. A man with a rock poorly glued to a machine gun in his guest room. The quiet house, barely occupied, sitting in a quiet town, too sad to rest.

For a moment I thought I heard a hand twisting the doorknob, but it was only the wind through the window jittering the hinges. I thumbed a Xanax from the bottle, washed it down with saliva, and wished for a bird to land in the window, for some distraction to clear my conscience.

I whispered, *There can be no true clearing, but it's fine anyway.*

--

This may or may not have been an anesthetic dream: After they removed the tumor, I couldn't help but ask, "May I see it? The little man?"

The doctor let me, but hesitantly.

Then I asked, "May I touch it?"

The doctor resisted at first, but then changed his mind.

He placed it in my palm and I held, momentarily, a delicate and lifeless thing. A mash of wrinkled cartilage and hair. Like a tennis ball stripped bald and rolled around in the gunk found in clogged faucets.

I thought: *You had a good go of it.*

I thought: *I don't want to end up like you.*

# 4

My skin there, how to describe it? What I found in the morning mirror, only three days in? A hint of sunburn across the bridge of my nose. The skin sagging, cracking and ballooning under my eyes, agitated by dry air and dust.

They have a saying in Gyumri—even the dust is covered in dust. I did what I could to combat it.

First washing my face well, then moisturizing, adding rice protein foundation with SPF 20, then rouge and mascara. It was something but couldn't possibly have been enough.

The shower at Levon's stayed cold. I either couldn't figure out the hot water or it just didn't work, so I bird bathed. Lapped it under my pits and between my legs. It, too, was something.

On my third morning in Armenia, I found Levon sitting in the dining room, playing solitaire on his computer. Hearing me he turned and rose from the table. "Melik will be to walk you. But first you come here."

I followed him to the kitchen, where he began grinding grounds into a coffee cup over the sink. Dressed for work, a spicy cologne wafted as he busied around the kitchen. He pointed to the kitchenette, said, "sit," and I complied, laying my easel against the kitchen wall and thanking him for the coffee he placed before me. I bowed my head into the delicate yellow cup and let it sink in that my quiet, compliant actions had me looking like a demure child away from their parents. It gave me a dull pang, a frustrated emptiness.

From the living room came sad piano music on morning television. I crooked my neck around to see a war montage, lit candles, soldiers marching, a parade of tanks, doves released into the gray air, a large bonfire in the countryside at sunset. Levon leaned against the sink and I heard him light a cigarette, felt him look my way. I kept my focus on the television as his smoke curled over my head. I heard him grind more coffee into the bottom of another cup, I heard the boiling water. The rhythm of Levon's morning. I tried not to appear too occupied with it.

Behind me, through the open window, a tangy smell of fire. I turned to find a woman below, burning a dead leaf pile, airing the flames with a sweeper pan. I'd read about these fires, these older women, burning leaves and carefully fanning the flames. Remnants of pagan times. The goal: be careful not to breathe too hard on the flames, not to spit on them, or to let a strand of hair fall, anything that might dirty the sacred. But to what end? I couldn't recall if I'd read to what end.

Levon stood at the table, pushed a crystal bowl of bruised plums my way, and grunted for me to take one. "One." He pointed to the bread, sliced and stacked in a neat pile. "Here, one, too." And I complied.

He sat across from me and sighed, a meaty sound with the phlegm of his throat. I thanked him and returned my eyes to the television in the living room, credits now rolling with the Star Wars theme, words over a black backdrop, white Armenian script moving fast out of frame.

As I chewed, I considered what to say or do, tempted to go to some girlish-innocent gesture, to look up at Levon and offer him a wedge of his own bread. To ask if he'd eaten. To ask him what his day held. Logical questions that hit each spot on a progressive path that might paint me as the good guest I aimed to be. But before I could begin he stabbed his cigarette into the ashtray and leaped up to his phone. He dialed a number, someone answered and he said something in the confident voice that ran out of him when speaking his language, when being himself. I let a sour resentment buzz through me for reasons I couldn't quite locate.

--

The heat of the sun at 10 a.m. peels you away from yourself. Makes your scars throb. But that day I remembered to carry water, at least.

I let Melik walk me to the Ghost Town, but insisted he take his leave from there, reluctantly agreeing to let him return after four hours. Before he left, I asked about the hammering he'd said I might hear coming from the buildings.

"Sometimes they die disassembling. People of the *domiks*. There are so many reasons to disassemble a building here. To repurpose materials, you know? But you should just stay away from the buildings." He shrugged his shoulders, "Sometimes they fall." He was wearing the same hat. He tipped it as he turned on his heels and walked toward the horizon line.

I notched in at the spot where I'd worked the day before, firm on making more progress and procrastinating less. All was as I'd left it. Same sun, same rosehips and yellow weeds, same broken structures still and quiet ahead. I dug out supplies and told myself to fret less about designated placements or organization, told myself that how I chose to lay the paints on the ground didn't matter as much as how I'd lay them on the canvas. Like an insomniac hoping for sleep at sunset, I hoped I wouldn't stop painting once I started.

So I started. I sketched out three thin black acrylic lines on a new canvas, mapped a study of angles. I tried to remain present, tried to capture sunlight as it changed with the day. Working fast enough to contain the fleeting image indifferent to my need to record it. Snatching it up before it changed and became something else altogether.

As a rule, the closer you drift toward evening the longer the shadows diffuse, spread over the scene and change the shade. In the field those problems seemed to thrive. The problems I wanted to harness lived in their natural elements. But other problems lurked, too. Like the challenge of time. In the field the hours lacked shape. Time had a thin watery texture. It flooded over the field.

Too much time in too wide a space, with such a long horizon. It was one thing to paint a building, but another to take on time and space itself.

I watched the thin black lines, the angles, and waited for them to tell me what to do. I pushed away and came back. I laid down color and the minutes barely budged.

My paint marks mocked the phases of light in the field, but to make well-defined links beyond this, to actually understand the object in context—I began to doubt it could happen. I couldn't truly say what was happening, I only knew I wanted something of the building before me to emerge.

I longed for a distraction, to see a rabbit or squirrel roam by, or a bird overhead, but nothing moved other than shadows under the westward sun.

I reminded myself that this was what I wanted. To be there and to do that. I'd asked for those amorphous hours. I ask for the opportunity to peel away from myself.

I lay back on the ground and watched the sky as the minutes dribbled. I beckoned myself inward, to a dim cavity.

Instructed myself to breath deep from my stomach. I went there and waited for something to collide with me. I tried to peek out and conjure the building in the picture, but realized I could no longer recall it clearly. My life felt oddly absent against the new landscape.

Then my father floated by. Not his face, I'd lost that years ago. It was a figure in the BDUs worn by Armenian soldiers on television, with some smudge of his face.

My father had always ignored my questions about what it was like to fly an F-15. I had asked him what it felt like to break the sound barrier, to explain that pinging that blossoms in your ear and the white smoke fanning around the jet at that moment.

"When you break it what happens to you up there?"

He said it wasn't that exciting. It feels like nothing. A flight suit designed to keep the blood from rushing away from your head contains you. Tilting up or down, the flight suit just gets tighter.

"Life's more exciting down here, when your blood is allowed to rush around," he said.

I never believed it, even at age five, but I believe he thought he was saying the right thing.

I peeked out from the cavity of me and shoved my father away. I took in the bright heat and tried to imagine the details of Narine's photo and couldn't.

That lack of imagining was a failure, the sort of slip-up that comes when losing the shape of the figures and images that make up your life.

I learned long before that life begins blurring almost as soon as you turn in another direction.

I thought about home and wondered who would still be awake. It would have been the middle of the night there. No doubt Eric was probably still working.

I stood and moved away from the canvas, walking a wide arc around the field. I thought about the buildings.

*Sometimes they die disassembling.*

*There are so many reasons to disassemble a building here.*

--

In those days before I left, Narine's bakery felt better than my apartment. It felt better than surrounding myself with the people who would claim to know me best, who claimed to know what I was doing wrong and needed to improve. Mostly people ordered and picked up their cakes and baklava and went, never sitting at one of the only two tables. That was one of the things I liked about it. Even when I'd sit for the better part of a day, Narine never seemed to mind. If anyone minded it was the boy I'd mistook to be her son. He'd flash me looks of suspicion from time to time, come over to empty the garbage and linger at my shoulder. He'd clear his throat and nod to the hours of operation sign when the day was done and the door was about to get locked behind me. It was never Narine who told me to leave, perhaps only because it was his job and not hers. But I never really felt bad because I'd order coffee after coffee and baklava after baklava. I never stayed without reason. I tried to earn my presence.

When I visited, Narine always had something to share about Armenia, perhaps making a point of priming me or perhaps just making conversation. I could never tell. Sometimes it was just an anecdote about Gyumri, but sometimes her stories thickened the room, shifting it to a darker, cooler hue. I'd visualize these stories, sometimes want to paint them large across the front of buildings, across whole cityscapes.

Two days before I boarded my flight, the same day a small red notch exposed itself from where the hard film of the suture glue was flaking away, I realized that it no longer hurt to cough or sneeze. I ordered tabbouleh, baklava and a coffee to go. Ringing up the order, Narine told me she never really left Gyumri.

She said, "No. Armenians never leave. It's a large, embracing shadow. It's a half-truth if not a whole one. Any Armenian will say."

I told her I thought that made sense.

Narine said, "No. We leave but we never leave the dead. Or, you could say, the dead never leave us. But things are the same everywhere. People are people and death is death. Yes?"

"Yes."

She packed the pint container of tabbouleh, placed the baklava in a brown bag and folded it over delicately. "The border between the living and the dead, it's a crazy line. But you know, far before the earthquake the days were always about the dead with Armenians. We've got our days of the dead, such holidays, but really the dead are every day. It's in the blood, to be with our dead. It's in our breath. It's what one means when they say: It's all I've ever known. It's in the bread we knead and the flowers we buy. The days belong to the dead, but they belong to us, too. Days begin and end this way."

"Wow," I said in place of nothing.

"You know about *Merlotz*?" She asked.

I didn't.

She explained, *Merlotz* is what Armenians call their day of the dead. The tradition of slaughtering a sheep was harder that first *Merlotz* after the earthquake. It felt wrong to hang life from the tree boughs that way. People were more sensitive to the trees after the earthquake. Sensitive to anything that hadn't fallen or broken into pieces. That year, that first *Merlotz*, some thought: no need for more carcasses. No need for more of that smell. No need for the eerie quiet that follows an animal's last jerk. And what to do with all the uneatable portions? But still sheep were slaughtered. It's the right thing to do, some said. Keeping in touch with tradition is healthy.

Narine recalled on that *Merlotz*, arguing with her family over whether or not God was still there. For the most part, the family agreed to disagree. Everyone walked even slower than usual on the way to the graves that year. Everyone was tired, more tired than usual. Tired of living with the dead.

Narine didn't tell me which side of the argument she was on and I didn't think to ask because I knew she'd have told me if she thought it important to share.

I remember thinking yes, the dead are tiring. As are the dead portions sliced from us. But the living can be tiring, too. I didn't say it and I hated myself for thinking it at all. I imagined how uncomfortable it would be if I tried to acknowledge what she'd been through as if I could relate.

--

I dropped my easel and supplies off at Levon's and told Melik, who paced around the kitchen eating a plumb, that I had it from there. I preferred to spend the afternoon walking on my own.

"Where will you go?"

"Not sure. Museums?"

"Yes, you must go to museums."

"I've heard this is true."

"Our museums will teach you the best, I can take you if you need." He picked plumb skin from his teeth.

"I got it."

"Of course. Museum of National Architecture and Urban Life. You just go down the hill, to the left on the street just past Vartanants Square and down the block some. Easy. I think it should not be too hard for you to find. Just look for the palace

*72*

building. I've got work today. Writing. Call me if you need anything."

I reminded him I had no phone but if I needed to I'd figure out a way to reach him.

"Museums," he said with distance in his voice, picking up another plumb from the dish. "The past doesn't walk the streets, but still moves in its own way."

I asked him whose quote that was and he said it was his. "Just wrote it in my story," he said proudly. It wasn't meant to be a joke but it made me laugh, which he didn't seem to mind. He was easy on me that way, forgiving of my misplaced laughter, I assumed because in his head he was already elsewhere.

--

Walking down the hill, nausea hit, reminding me I hadn't eaten. At a small store, I navigated tight rows of potatoes, watermelon and shiny bags of candy. The lights were out and I couldn't tell if it was just the store or everywhere—both seemed equally possible.

I remembered the rock on the gun, a thought that tightened my chest, and looked around for something resembling glue or anything else strong enough to affix a rock to the back of a machine gun, but found nothing.

A shopkeeper walked in from an adjacent room, wearing an unseasonably heavy brown sweater, offering me only a numb expression as he assessed my foreignness. I said hello in English as a way of saying, *don't worry, I'm not capable of engaging you, and even if my life were in danger it would be hard to ask you for help.* I cleared my throat and pointed to the cheese and bread I wanted inside the glass case below the counter and grabbed a can of what I took to be ice coffee, a brown aluminum can covered in smiling, dancing coffee beans. He used his calculator to tab up the purchases and pointed to the amount. I handed over exact change and said thank you in his language. He winced out a smile.

Outside, the sun was westward now and the day's heat and dust had settled into the sweat of my skin. I doused my nausea with the sweet milky coffee. My head weighed more than a head should ever weigh.

I passed Vartanants Square, walked through a bazaar dodging eye contact, keeping my head down to the worn out dusty bricks, rows of open rice bags, spilling over with nuts and spices, crates of greens, brilliantly red pomegranates, a pile of furs strewn over a canvas.

Two men repairing the ornate stones in the sidewalk, paused their saws as I passed. I moved by fast, my face fixed on the world in front of me, as though I was headed somewhere important.

--

A couple days before I left for Armenia, Frannie called to see how I was doing. I cradled the phone between my shoulder and ear, lifted my shirt in the bathroom mirror and told her I couldn't be better. I bit back asking her why she'd mentioned my infertility to Eric. It wasn't worth it, but the emotion leaked out.

"Sarcasm won't heal you any faster," she said.

My abdomen had almost deflated back in place, the gash darkening. I flaked the last of the surgical glue from around the spot and for a moment thought to tell her where I was going. I was just about to, but stopped. I needed things obstacle free. I knew if just one person told me not to go then I wouldn't. And that was something I couldn't allow.

"You're right as usual," I said in a patronizing tone I knew would get her.

--

It was Narine that had told me I needed to go to the Museum of National Architecture and Urban Life. She explained it as the house of a wealthy family, built back when houses were built to last in Gyumri, therefore coming out of the quake unscathed. Google had confirmed it as the Dzitoghtsyan family's 19th century home, a sprawling compound of gold and gray tuff stones in the era of Belle époque architecture.

Past the French lace iron entrance, inside a cavernous hall, a woman with a face of heavy pale makeup sat reading a newspaper behind a small desk. After a fast scan she pointed to a cardboard sign propped on the desk that said 500 dram. I handed over the money and she slipped a bookmark shaped ticket out of her desk drawer—an image of the building itself—and placed it in my hand. When she closed the desk, the sound jumped off the walls, the only real sound in the transaction, a sound that said *please move on.*

The damp coolness of the museum's entrance hall brought relief from the sun, followed fast by a new awareness of just how much I'd sweated through my clothes. I needed to wash my face and wished I'd done so at Levon's. Looking around the long hall I saw nothing but the desk and the wordless woman now back to her newspaper. "Restroom?" I asked. Without looking up, she pointed ahead, down the long, dark hall.

I moved down the hall and the lights buzzed on, filling the room before me with an anemic glow, a wallpapered room of roped off furniture tableaus, velvet backed chairs. In the corner stood a woman, a museum guard, whose job duties included controlling the lights. She dodged eye contact but I sensed her monitoring me as I passed the displays of dining room sets and antique wardrobes, tea pots, stoves, hung woven rugs, ornamental cribs, writing tables, eye specs resting atop a book, embroidered tablecloths and pillowcases, a gramophone and large mantel mirror, some sober paintings and photographs—portraits of poets, story tellers, folk actors, musicians. Objects placed in a logical way that spoke to some living past.

One narrow room led into another. I came to a corridor, lined with Plexiglas cases, each containing the remnants of dresses on headless mannequins. Through the reflection of the Plexiglas I saw my puffiness, my sunburn. One room held nothing but black cases of silver jewelry, old hammers, and blacksmithing tools. Each room had its own woman in control of the lights, each with its own collection of carefully placed artifacts and narratives of suffering, resilience and minutia. The wall captions had no English translation, so it was only because of Narine that I could say the museum consisted of antiques cleared from the rubble after 1988. Objects salvaged, put back together again, or not shattered or broken. Spared objects speaking to the one-time owners, whoever they were. Famous and average citizens, people who might have moved and died elsewhere—to the Caucuses, Russia, Paris, Yerevan, prison.

I was taken more with the women who controlled the lights than the objects they guarded. Some in heels and makeup and some less primped. All were young. Mostly they avoided locking eyes, but when I did catch them, which I strained to do, I smiled, and they limply, shyly, briefly smiled back before casting their gaze elsewhere, reverting to their heavy expressions of boredom, or fatigue, or depression, or whatever made their faces sad.

I finally found the bathroom through a thin door off to the side by the exit. The light didn't work and I was fine with feeling in the dark if it meant avoiding the sight of my face. I dabbed my cheeks with a wet towel, bringing to life the full sting of the settling sunburn.

I exited through the end of the tunnel and a woman sweeping the floor didn't look up as I passed.

--

Before I got to Gyumri I learned from Wikipedia that the face on the 10,000 dram belongs to a poet named Avetik Isahakyan. A poet who joined the Armenian Revolutionary Federation and got arrested a year later. After his release, he wrote a collection of poems and called them "Songs and Wounds." People referred to the poems as a sorrowful capturing of the injustices of life. He would go on to get arrested several more times and was eventually arrested for alleged actions against Russia's Tsar. He was sent to Odessa where he wrote more. When he got out it wasn't long before they arrested him again. The poet was well known for freezing moments or images in place. The poet believed that words are certain, always predictably measured, worthy of trust and never too precious.

I also read the story of another poet who they called Shiraz. In 1914, a woman's husband is killed by Turks and days later her son is born and given up for adoption. Those tasked with the orphan's care quickly baptized him in Gyumri's Church of the Seven Wounds. When he was old enough to run he began to run away. By age 7 he found his mother, hanging laundry for money. Together they lived in a basement. Everything they owned went dank and mildewed. For money and to pass the days he scooped water from the spring whatever way he could and sold what didn't spill to anyone on the street who would take it. When he grew up he took to writing poems. Some said his poems smelled like roses covered in morning dew and he didn't mind hearing this. He wrote 8000 lines about genocide and the Soviets banned them. The town of Gyumri gave him a six-roomed house as a gift. He died before he could live in it.

I walked and thought of these wonderful and dead men, who must have been among the faces in the photographs pinned to the museum walls. It must have been their objects on display, roped off, under lights controlled by young, sleepy-faced women. They were all people that knew disaster. All I could do was see it from the other side of the rope. How strange for me to see it at all.

I recognized my disasters were small when compared with what people faced throughout most of the world, certainly in Gyumri, but I knew my small disasters amounted to something. Small clumps of havoc to maneuver around. Small commotions to dodge. Small disappointments hit face-on. I felt it in my groin as I walked. An intermittent stab with each swing of the left leg. Some new pain? I was too close to it. And the blister threatened to return.

I carried my pain to the Russian restaurant on Vartanants Square. I punctured the scene, plopping into a wooden booth by the window. The restaurant became the restaurant with the foreign girl. The few patrons shifted around in their seat to see for themselves. The girl sat alone, staring at a menu she'd never learn to read.

A server dashed over, the same server as the night before, her short hair died a fading fuchsia, her thin lips a hot red. She smiled the broad smile of recognizing a returning customer. Something about the fine cracks that crinkled at her eyes made me think she was younger than she looked.

I asked for the one dish I knew I could say—borsch. "Borsch," the server repeated with slow concentration. Then a chain of other words, more rapidly delivered, that I gauged formed a question, a reflection of her hoping for more than I had. I gave only my blank face, the muscles of it soft, and some vague apology under my breath. She retreated, returning fast with borsch, bread, greens and a plate of potatoes I hadn't ordered. She retreated fast again.

I sat across from a table of three older men. They drank Gyumri brand beer and sat cross-legged, each with the large slouching heads of Gyumri men. I waited for them to cackle into laughter at my expense, my stomach fluttered with anticipation of it, but they kept low voices. They kept to their quiet, stony ways. I resisted watching them directly, letting my eyes go only from my bowl to the window, the taxis pulling up and pulling out, slight signs of functioning commerce on the street. I swirled the beet juice, spooned out the purple beef and ate fast to punctuate my purpose. I was there only to eat. My presence had to do with utility.

Even so, I kept catching the table of men looking at me. The one with his back to me, an abnormal head, pointy and flat, whipped around from time to time in a way I couldn't miss.

They laughed abruptly as though a joke had been made. As though I was the joke. But most likely I wasn't the joke, I knew that deep down. Whatever it was that had these men so focused on me it likely only lived in my head, in my fluttering stomach, in my sunburn, in the stab at my groin that slept as I sat, in the blister growing at my heel, waiting for me to walk.

But I resented them anyway, a table of men at ease. On them I deposited all things negative I'd carried to their country and through the door of their restaurant. I ate as fast as I could, eager to get away from them.

--

I believed myself capable of feeling out the general direction from the restaurant back to Levon's, of retracing my steps, but found myself travelling a semi-circle. So I turned and walked the opposite direction and reminded myself to breathe. The stabbing in my groin and the blister remained quiet as though they'd agreed to let up so I could get where I needed to go. The sun was mostly gone, and in its place night began dribbling down. The only sounds came from the other side of windows. Swatches of kitchen scenes, clanking dishes in sinks, steam on a square of glass and dull amber light. Other than those faint signs of human order there was only the crunch of my feet over gravel and fear bubbling to the surface. I imagined my own grim news, images of my lifeless limbs poking from a heap of rocks behind a house, filling televisions and streaming on laptops. But I came back around in my head, remembering Armenia's crime rate was low compared to home. And Narine said herself—that kind of danger isn't one of Gyumri's daily worries. But then the wild dogs were real, I figured. Probably. Wild dogs that'll eat anything? I hadn't read anything about dogs, but why would Melik lie?

I felt through the night, pausing for a minute to consider my course, and chose to retrace my steps back to the square before I managed to kick up more panic.

But then I changed my mind and told myself I could do it. I told myself that Gyumri required feeling around in the dark and occasionally getting knocked off course. It required feeling like you were the joke when probably you weren't. I'd asked for it. I chucked myself into the world, the main figure in a composition of my own making. I *could* walk back. So I set off again, this time taking the road just left of the square, heading the right direction.

Within a few blocks, the darkness enveloped me and the streetscape dissolved altogether, the right direction wasn't so right anymore. It was too dark to continue. I turned around again.

Walking back, defeated by night, my thoughts turned to my father as they often did when my head hit a fear trap. My father breaking the sound barrier, jerking the earth with an F-15, leaving that pinging in the eardrums of everyone he passed over. Sometimes it could convince me the fear was not worth the effort.

But I had my mother's impulse to shrink, her meekness. That meekness reminded me that a body moving in the world is a delicate thing. And it's so easy for something to go wrong. It's a horror to think too much about it, and it's a horror easy to think about. It's amazing my mother and father ever got together at all.

I walked down the middle of the dark, Gyumri road, head to ground looking for holes and jagged rocks, anything that could break me, and eventually light appeared. A streetlight, then a series of them. The one patch of that friable city, well lined with electricity, where people walked and cars moved. The Russian restaurant, the broken church, the slumped evergreens with old Christmas decor. My body unclenched and I let out a long, hard breath.

I approached the first taxi I saw, a silver Toyota. In the driver's seat, a young man with spiky blond hair, and the hard, unmalleable mouth of his town. He raised his arm sluggishly, as though to shrug a *what-gives?* gesture and I fumbled into my bag, pulling out my notebook and, believing it more efficient to point than utter words, pointed to Levon's address. He took hold of the notebook and studied it for a long time before returning it and nodding to the back seat. A shaky pit of embarrassment rolled through my gut, but I kept a loose expression as I got in the car. To come off casual. To say this was nothing at all. "Thanks," I said in English.

*Thanks.* It came out horrible. It came out flailing, with no coordination. I could have said this word in Armenian and set a different tone. I might have passed for knowing something of the language. I might have looked more legitimate.

In the front passenger seat sat another man, with similar spiky blond hair. Neither turned to engage me, which I took as a best-case scenario. The car was started and loud techno came over the stereo, drowning out their conversation. Even though I couldn't understand them, I strained to make out their words, the tone and cadence, to detect some signal of whether I should worry for my safety, whether the safer option wasn't to walk a questionable course in the dark. They talked in short clips like people at ease, which I took as a good sign.

Only blocks from the square, less than two minutes in, we reached the lit road of Tigran Mets, Levon's street. I waved my arm between the front seats. "Here here here!" The driver slammed the brake, not bothering to pull over to the side of the road, and his friend lowered the music. Both turned to look squarely at me. I offered a 10,000-dram bill, the smallest bill I could fish from my pocket, about 20 US dollars, and said thank you in Armenian. The driver took my money with a nod, turned around and offered no change. The passenger turned the stereo back up, confirming the exchange was over. They had cheated me as I had expected and allowed, and all that was left to do was climb silently from the car.

I stopped at a small grocer near Levon's house and pulled two bottles of Gyumri brand beer from the refrigerator. The woman behind the counter wore an *I love New York T-Shirt*. She smiled when I pointed at her chest, gave a thumbs up and said "New York!" My excitement wasn't ironic and it surprised me to be so grateful for such a small thing.

I turned to find Melik standing behind me.

"Coincidence!"

"No. Not really, I followed you," he said, shrugging his shoulders, his endearing tic.

"Followed from where?" I sounded as defensive as I felt. Gyumri cracked me in new ways. The grip had a new feel. The constrictions arrived as new sensations.

Melik explained that Levon had called him asking if he knew where I was and when Melik said he didn't, Levon suggested he go find me. At first Melik said, no, that would be crazy, but then decided he should, just in case, you never know.

He was headed toward the square, assuming I'd be there, but then there I was walking up Tigran Mets. He shrugged again. "Tomorrow I can help you buy a sim card and phone if you want. It shouldn't be expensive by your standards."

I handed him a beer, said, "No thank you, but here's a beer, feel free."

--

The three of us sat at Levon's picnic table, drinking beer from small juice glasses. Levon had laid carpets over the benches and poured sunflower seeds in a ceramic plate. I sat across from Melik and Levon, the two of them chain smoking, cross-legged. They spoke mostly to each other, which didn't bother me at all. From their body language, I tried guessing what they might be saying, but I had no clues to piece together the puzzle. I took the job of keeping our small glasses full seriously, to have a purpose. The air was almost not hot and the beer was all right.

Melik waved his hand to get my attention. "Levon is proud of his courtyard. Last year he removed a *domik* house from this square plot here, once the family there left for Russia. He planted flowers and now it is greener than anywhere in town."

"I believe it," I said. "It's a great yard."

Levon is a good and popular man in this town." Levon kept his eyes to his knees. Melik patted him on the back and murmured something in Armenian. "For example," Melik continued, "he once talked a friend out of kidnapping his future wife because the practice is out of fashion."

"Well, that's good."

"Unfortunately it is still in fashion sometimes but good people make efforts. So Levon wants me to explain, I mean, to translate, the story of the earthquake, his experiences. He believes you want to know."

Of course I wanted to know but it embarrassed me to think I might have somehow expressed as much, might have inadvertently done or said something to express morbid curiosity about Levon's earthquake losses or traumas. I shrugged casually, said, "Sure."

Levon began to speak, with Melik translating.

"When it began happening he ran from the 9th floor to the first floor of the factory he was working in. People thought it was a bomb but then slowly they realized. So, first he ran to his mother who was teaching at a school and she was there and everything was okay with her. So then he went to his father and his uncle and they were okay. Then he was driving to his aunt's house and when he got close to the building, he could see it ahead collapsing. He tried to help but there were heavy stones too big to lift. It is not easy to take apart a building after it falls. His uncle's wife, his aunt, was only there from the legs down. And his sister, they could not find her. He lost his sister—the one of the three sisters he liked. Right after the earthquake he says he had so much energy and this helped him to go looking for his sister, for anyone, really. That first night came fast because the sun went down faster than usual. Like the sun didn't want to be there. They lit candles and kept digging. Him and everyone dug and listened for living sounds under rocks and bricks. Mostly they heard nothing. Eventually they realized that nothing could be done without a crane, so the government brought cranes from Yerevan. With the cranes they could lift the beams. They found a woman who'd lost a hand and once they lifted the beam she got out and she was running and he never saw her again. They worked in shifts and all day and night. The military came but they really only knew what to do in a bomb explosion, not an earthquake. Everyone realized fast that you must be like a surgeon to remove someone from a fallen building. And it is not easy to be that careful. It took a crowd of many men. After some days the crowd lost their energy at night but then the sun would come again and they would work hard. When they found a body they congratulated each other. No matter how destroyed the body was. For many months after that he lived in the factory where he had worked. The building was mostly okay. 1988 was a time border. Everything was under the earthquake. Everything spoiled. Friendship left. People left. Most people couldn't take it, living with just a plate and a knife. Being forced to make something out of rubble. The government promised supplies but the trains never arrived. There was a blockade with Azerbaijan and the Soviets did not keep their promises. Eventually, they started to build new houses outside the city limits. Nobody had much petrol. Trade embargoes made it hard to find good food and medicine, and everyone fought. And what little there was to buy was too expensive. And people were not always good, unfortunately. Some would go into destroyed buildings and steal everything. They walked over bodies to get to things. They sprayed their machine guns in the air for no reason. Just to let out anger. And for some years this was normal. That first year, somehow, people got through the winter, a spring, a summer and then when winter was coming again people became worried about what it might bring. It was not easy. And now. These new buildings. No one believes they will stand if nature does that shit again."

--

I climbed on the bed, tried again to balance the rock on the gun. If only I could sink it back in the wedge of glue. But it was hopeless. I lay on the bed, contemplating taking a Xanax. I tried to convince myself not to. With a dwindling supply, I calculated I'd have just enough to fly home. I broke one in half. Then a door at the opposite end of the hall opened, Levon's bedroom door, a signifier he might go to bed. I sat up, waiting for anything beyond the door. The smell of his smoke or the creaking of his hallway floor as his heavy legs lumbered past. Nothing. To think of him sleeping, rather than up all night, relaxed me. Perhaps it was the beer.

After some silence, I unclicked the door and moved along the hall, down the stairwell to the basement, pausing midway, waiting for Levon to stir. Nothing.

I switched the basement light on, scanning the walls for a tube or a jar of something that might affix the rock to the gun. Industrial glue, rubber cement, an adhesive. I peeked through drawers and closets, handling the knobs as quiet as I could, tapping as light as possible. I found papers, clothes, board games missing covers, a jar of tacks. In the garage I searched for the light switch, running my hand along the wood grooves, the cool smell of wet grass coming through the open garage window, just the faintest buzzing of night bugs.

Then came the creek above and my name. I moved fast into the house, easing the lock behind me, leaning against the bathroom door, answering up, as casual as I could muster. "I was just going to the bathroom, Levon, good night."

Levon's voice barreled down. "You go outside? "

"No, I'm here. It's fine."

I locked myself in the bathroom and turned the light on, turned the water on, went through motions that kept my lie on track.

# 5

Again, Melik in the kitchen and me bleary eyed and grasping for the coffee Levon extended as I entered the room. Again, Levon dressed for work. His wet, parted hair, his heavy cologne and stiff slacks. I went through the anticipated gestures, sitting in my usual spot, tearing a piece of bread from the loaf, chirping out something predictable about the weather, the taste of the bread and the coffee. Then, turning to Melik, "If you walk me to the Ghost Town again today I will make you stay and I will paint you."

From behind his coffee cup, Melik replied with his usual nonchalance, "That's fine, I have the morning."

I'd half hoped my request might deter him from going, might be what was needed to scare him away. But then I considered how his presence could be used. To add a human subject might be just what I needed to add some structure to the hours. So I pressed on and asked, "Then could you wear the shirt you had on yesterday? The black and white stripes?"

--

Melik asked why I preferred to paint between the hours of 10 and 1 and I explained how it's the hours of strongest light. "The sun moves with the day and so the shadows spread as the day goes. The light weakens," I said, "and the sun here, it's so strong. No trees, no clouds. Just sun. It's amazing. But still, even with all this daylight, you just get a small window when it's as good as it's going to get. Basically after 1ish, it's all just dulling light."

I set up my easel in what I was starting to consider my spot. An impression had settled into the steppe from the last few days, the dehydrated stems of dull yellow and purple flowers permanently crunched. I loved the idea of claiming a place and physically shaping the earth, even if I knew nobody was challenging me to seize it.

I tossed down my supplies, having abandoned all ideas of spreading things out in a logical order, and ordered Melik to the desired distance, some 15 feet away, wanting him at a scale that felt right. "Stay turned away. Face toward the buildings."

"Why?" He asked.

"Because."

"You don't want to paint my face?"

"No."

"Why?"

"Well, at the risk of sounding melodramatic, I just don't want to capture anything that might be in your face. I don't want to have to figure out what to do with what runs under your skin."

As the hours crept, the field maintained its stillness. Melik sat on his side, back to me. With his figure, a new vibration entered the square of canvas. With Melik, a warmness presented itself, new shape and color to contend with. I fostered the aluminum white of him, the Naples yellow and ochre, I put his black in slow.

Melik yelled to me, "What's so interesting to you about painting?" His words in the wind, telling me I wasn't alone. The landscape was now human and to stay focused I reminded myself I'd invited this humanness.

I yelled back, "What's not interesting about painting? I mean, what's interesting is you don't— well, you will never see the same colors twice. Sorry, but try not to move around too much."

I was like my sister, barking orders, desperate to arrest a situation. I got a pang of longing, thinking of Frannie out there, unplanned thoughts suddenly there, floating up from the dark cavity, a strange pulsing in my gut. I linked it to Frannie, the sudden discomfort. I was prone to somatic responses when it came to her.

--

The east coast was a prickly cold when my mother, sister and I arrived from Alamogordo, just after Christmas. We stayed at our uncle's house—my mother's brother—in the low ceilinged basement apartment of his cul-de-sac house, and were due to stay until our father beckoned us to Germany, his next assignment, once an apartment opened up on the base. My sister and I had met our uncle only once before. And even under his roof, we barely saw him. I came to believe, though I'd no proof, that his absence was inevitably the fault of my mother. I'm not sure we were ever welcome there.

I still don't know the exact day that my mother found out my father's brain had decided to quit on him. I never found out who it was that delivered the news or how they did it. In time I would learn he died only a week after arriving in Germany. But she didn't tell us about it for nearly a month.

Since there was never a clear timeframe for us to move to Germany, it was easy for her to ward off my questions as to how long we'd be staying there.

I have a foggy recollection of how those days were spent. I sketched the skeletal limbs of the trees that lined the slit of a window, near the ceiling. Mother lay on the couch and watched the *Price is Right*. Her lidded tumbler held coffee and whiskey. Frannie was barely walking. Barely off my mother's lap. In my memory of it, we never leave the room. In my memory we get no more of the outside world than intermittently lifting our heads to the slits of that one window, the view of those skeletal trees. The damp room remained dim through all the day's hours. Scratchy blankets lay everywhere. Sometimes my mother would rise to refill her tumbler. I've still got the smell of that cup. That sour wafting from the spills that lay in various stages of dry on the floor.

But mostly my mother would keep my sister on her lap, my sister not even two. And that was the first time I felt uneasy about Frannie. The sausage feet and the smug, sleepy expression, the red cheeks. I hated how at ease she was laying in our mother's arms. I blamed her for holding us down. A weight that kept us from going out in the world. My mother and I would be more mobile without her fat baby body to worry about. She was the reason we never really went anywhere.

At night with Frannie and my mother asleep, I kept the TV buzzing, sat close to hear the low mumble. The only show I remember: reruns of The New Twilight Zone, a frazzled housewife named Penny found a relic in her basement and by carrying it in her pocket could make the world freeze just by saying shut up. She found quiet by freezing and unfreezing the world on command. But then as night came, those steely stars in her sky became nuclear weapons, just short of landing on earth. Penny yelled shut up, freezing the weapons above her head, freezing the world just before impact.

I can't recall that bridge between our days in that room and moving out and starting school. There is a gap in my memory between learning about my father's death, and getting on with my life.

But eventually the memories expand. They gain the nuance of life in the not-so-distant past. There was a new place to live. A brighter, multi-roomed apartment that threatened to lean toward cheery once the furniture accumulated. My sister learned new words. My mom intermittently left the house to work a vague customer service job that she complained had her talking so much she was sick of the sound of her own voice by day's end. The occasional visits of family. Then the presence of a new man. Charlie. Chubbier and shorter and louder than my father, as though she'd gone lengths to find someone his opposite.

My sister's memory of those days is non-existent. She'd always say she remembered nothing of those days in the dark box, the realization that our father's death. Nothing of the bare trees out the slit in the wall. Nothing of her fat docile body on my mother's lap, so complacent to stay still and coddled. In some ways her life hadn't started yet. In some ways she'd been spared.

--

That unease that was my sister inside me, the heat of Gyumri, I paused and put my head between my legs, thinking a fainting spell was near.

Then Melik snapped me back to the field.

"Sitting this way, on my side. I can't feel my leg now."

--

I painted Melik for as long as the light would allow and then we parted ways. I found myself at the town center and there I met Emma, an Armenian American experimental filmmaker from Los Angeles, in the country for 7 weeks to "restart her clock," having previously lived there for a few years (she couldn't remember exactly how many) until 2009, when she abruptly returned to the states for a family emergency. Emma spotted me on Mayisyan Street, between rows of crated grapes, nuts and sinewy root vegetables, pointed my way and proclaimed loudly how she knew an American when she saw one. There was something refreshing about her sudden appearance, the clear-ring of her American English. I accepted her enthusiastic invitation to find a place to sit and talk.

We drank yogurt water served from a large glass jug in a café. Delicate-boned and nymph-like, Emma was larger in presence than stature. A strange mix: elegantly pretty, despite the squeal-pitch of her voice and the anxious way she monkeyed in the chair.

I stayed within myself debating whether or not I liked her and she stayed engrossed with explaining her interest in the intersections between art and seismic effects, the enforcement of building codes, the integrity of structures, superficial inspections and construction that doesn't conform to approved, bureaucratic design. Emma asked, "I mean how could you *not* be interested in such things in a place like this?" I looked at her and blinked, at first not registering she'd just posed a question. When she continued without waiting for an answer, her words blending into a dense and at times undecipherable mass, I was glad not to be called on for much.

She went on about the shoddy fixes made by tenants to already weak and hastily built buildings. She called this the fast track to building deterioration and the compromise to seismic reliability. "Armenia's at an unusually high risk of exposure to natural disaster. Not just earthquakes, but hail and mudslides, you name it. Poverty equals an inability to protect yourself. I mean, right? That goes for *anywhere* not just here. But this place, this place. I mean that's why I decided I needed to come back now. In part to film, sure, but more so because when I left, I just felt like something got left behind. When I was here before, as a volunteer, I really discovered some missing piece of me, something ripped apart from me at birth. And now, when I'm not here, I feel diluted. Whatever it is, that piece of me I find here, it can't seem to make the trip back to the States."

Emma halted her monologue, concentrated on my face, her eyebrows up and her mouth curling into a smirk. I worried she thought I wasn't paying enough attention, that I'd offended her. But then she went on, after a dramatic pause, "Tell me about *your* project."

Ill prepared for a transition to speaking-role, I began telling Emma about the picture in the bakery and the painting in progress. My words failed to come together right, so I kept it sparse and tapered off quick, punctuating with, "It's complicated I guess."

Emma squinted, "I can dig it, though it's crazy to only work in such a narrow window. I mean, only being here for like a week or so? *Wild* really. I love the idea of such restraint on process, though."

Her eyes trailed off somewhere and in the silence I thought about contributing something rather than waiting for her to continue. Something, maybe, about artistic process or restraint or time. But I'd gotten used to listening to Emma, rather than talking to her, and preferred to wait for the natural shift of the conversation back in her direction. I suspected she did, too.

She eventually snapped from her distant stare and let out a cackle, rubbed her hand through her black pixie hair and called out to the waitress who conspicuously watched from the corner. Emma ordered something off the menu, or maybe asked for the check, then leapt back to English. "How fascinating. I mean you aren't even Armenian. Not knowing the language or *anything*. That, my dear, takes *balls*."

It ran against the grain of the day to have someone new in front of me, someone new to be answering to. It tapped the feral side of me, that bit prone to sensations of entrapment. But as patronizing as her words sounded, as agitating as her happiness was, and despite all my silent scrutinizing, there was something inherently likeable about her. I watched her large, darting eyes, and the twitchy muscles of her pretty face as she talked and I detected nothing but sincerity and a rare, unfiltered joy.

She said, "Doing projects is not a challenge here, *Jesus*, but it can be a challenge to narrow down what you want to do. It's funny. Two thousand people a year are leaving this country and who the hell are those of us who come back? Artists! We come for the opportunities. Opportunities to live cheaply and to express ourselves. I mean last week in Yerevan I met some people of the Diaspora here, self-funded photographers, who actually said, this was their words: that they want to capture the whole country. From ancient to modern. I mean what's *that* look like? Right? I'm thinking of maybe turning to straight up documentary work. Doing something about government corruption and housing. More grants in that. Seems though that some people are hesitant to speak up too much about those kind of political topics. The Soviet mindset is still very alive. But, anyway it can be hard to know what the fuck you are looking for. You know?"

I told her I knew.

"Of course you know. You are here after all. Well, have you been to the *domik* villages yet? You know, where the shanties are?"

"No. I mean yes; I know of them but haven't really gone."

"Well then I have an idea," she arched an eyebrow.

"Oh I don't know about that."

"But you *have* to!" She pleaded, in mock desperation, slapping her palms on the table like a child, an act I could tell she was accustomed to using. Something about her dramatic pleading led me to believe her motivation for latching on had to do with just this—a plotted out hunt for someone to take to the *domiks*, so she wouldn't have to go alone. I considered saying no out of spite. I considered that she put something ugly on display and now I had a reason to dislike her. And she might have sensed these considerations, might have read them in some slight shift of my expression, because she tightened her posture and began to explain that there are things at the *domiks* she needed to get on film before making her 8 p.m. ride back to Yerevan.

"I'll pay for the taxis. I'd just love the company. And it's something you can't not see," Emma said. Then she slipped back toward childish, propping her elbows on the table, cupping her head in her hands, locking her large eyes on me and finally shutting up to wait for my yes.

--

There is a relief that comes with letting go, with following, with letting someone else flag the taxi that sweeps you down the same maze of gravel streets you fumbled through the night before. In such moments you can go a little weightless, unruffled.

Emma in the front seat, her voice loud and large, bantered with the driver, whose hiccupping laugh said he was immediately endeared to her. And how could he not be? Emma bounced back and forth between whatever they were talking about and whatever she had to say to me. I imagined it was part of that missing piece she found there—the straddling of two worlds, her utter command of them both and the speed at which she could orbit around them, move between them. I envied it more than I envied her beauty or joy.

She sat backwards in her seat and hugged her knees. "After the earthquake, my mom came to my bedroom and said to go in my closet and pull out all the clothes I didn't want. I remember looking up at her and how frantic she was. I didn't understand what it meant. And even after she explained the earthquake I don't know that I totally got it. I remember I made a card and I wrote on it 'from your friend, I am sorry.' But I kept working at the card and couldn't quite get it perfect and my mom ended up shipping off supplies without it because I was taking too long. I was so upset. I asked my mom, what about my card and she said the card was not that important. And I'd wanted to come here ever since. Oh so, there is this town not too far from here where I was filming yesterday. A gold mining town. Species are dying from the shit that's going in the river. And fauna, greenery, but not just that, now the drinking water is fucked and of course anything that grows from the ground. So the village, they used to say: 'at least we have a job. We have no life but we have a job.' Guess what? The job pays less than any job in Yerevan. They give them as little as possible and of course what they pay later in birth defects and other health issues is much more."

She turned around to the driver, said something in Armenian, then switched to English, "So it's a con game. And you've heard this too, but don't give up. We have to fix this, this terrible corruption. And it's possible."

The driver offered a confused smile, met my eyes through the rearview mirror. I smiled brightly back, a feeble attempt to rise up to Emma's energy. His dismissive nod told me he wasn't convinced; I hadn't reached high enough to meet either of them wherever they were in the moment. Emma said something Armenian and the driver's response made her laugh. Emma translated that the driver didn't believe change was possible.

They laughed in unison and so I followed along, laughing, too, the three of us laughing at terrible things.

We passed rusting metal umbrellas on the side of the road, what looked like a gas station with camels tied up with ropes, houses in various degrees of completion and depletion, stones randomly strewn, a rusted out bus frame. Few cars were on the road. We passed the Russian barracks, its chicken wire fences, and another square with more statues—a square I'd walked past coming from the bus just days earlier.

Recognizing landmarks told me I'd hit a growth spurt of sorts. I'd learned something. To recognize a tiny speck on the surface. But slumped in the back of that taxi, it was enough to spark fleeting thoughts of securing a grant to come back. To do a series of paintings. Perhaps the whole of Ghost Town, perhaps animals, the wild dogs and camels at the gas station. From the back of the car on familiar roads, things felt possible, no matter how unmoored I remained.

--

We walked down a dirt road lined with *domiks* vacant of people, no noise save the faint squawk of passing birds and wind through weeds. In the distance a cracked bowl of concrete, an empty Soviet-era fountain, left a trace of once-significant but now-dead infrastructure.

Emma extended her camera to arm's length as we walked, a stylishly small, orange object I was glad to find so unimposing. I'd feared the dents and dings her filming might leave on what we found. How could it be welcomed?

She panned over a metal container bolted down by scalloped siding, fenced in with stretched mattress coils and metal grates, everything rusted and sharp. She explained, her voice softer and lower now, "This particular village was temporary housing for people working on rebuilding efforts and their families. People are still living in them. They were supposed to stay two years here, but it's been twenty-some. And over there, a school. A lot of students died." Emma nodded beyond the fountain, toward the stone-chunks resting beneath the remnants of a four-story structure. The sky spanning behind, pinked toward evening.

"And there, the town's veterinarian's home, or a zoologist, I'm not sure which, something like that." She pointed at a structure not far from the school. A nearly identical building of cream colored squares eaten out in chunks, the top right corner stuffed up with tires and plastic and the floor sagging, giving the window frames beneath an inverted arch.

Emma lifted her camera above her head, zoomed to the top right corner of the veterinarian's/zoologist's building, said "I'm just amazed at how these homes are pieced together. Pieces of things that have no business getting put together. Right now it's warm and there aren't big problems, but when it becomes colder and they don't have anything to heat their houses, that's when things get dicey. 12,000 people!" Emma managed to exert her enthusiasm without raising her voice, leaving me with hope we'd get to the other side without upsetting too my people.

Then, from a slit in a small tin can of a house, came a ruddy-faced woman in fuzzy blue slippers, her salt and pepper hair swooped back in a pompadour. She approached, said something, squinting up at our faces, perhaps perplexed, perhaps very pissed. Emma responded, kept the camera steady on the woman's face, and the woman said something back, turned to me, scratched her head and laughed.

Emma translated. "She thought maybe we were here to see the children. She says her grandchildren are studying in a boarding school because it's impossible for them to live here.

There's no water, nothing, so the kids stay at school as much as possible."

The woman pointed beyond us. Another woman now stood in her yard. She waved and we waved back, Emma said something loud and bright. I wondered if she'd met them before.

Emma translated, "So, she told me they just put up this mesh barrier made from a mattress frame because they are afraid for the children at night—when they come back from school for visits."

I let some desire to engage, some stupid question, fly from my mouth. "What is she afraid will happen?"

"Rats and wild dogs." Emma continued, "They have rabbits and pigeons they raise in small cages to have meat for the children in winter. She's blind in one eye. She says they're waiting for someone named Vaughn to bring wood. Soon it'll be winter and they don't have money to buy any wood.

"She has lots of debts in the shop. She owes too much money to buy anything. If she has to, she'll burn all the clothes she owns. I think she thinks we should know Vaughn because I guess he's someone who comes here a lot with foreigners?

"She owns the village grocery store. Every day she goes over her ledger of credits more full than the cash box. One person takes on credit, another pays back a debt and gradually she pays back the suppliers. They all call the store: 'A Poor Shop for a Poor Life.'"

Emma had never met these women, I came to realize, and from that point I started rationalizing how much money I should give, or if giving anything might be a faux pas. Another woman walked up and then a man behind her. They stood at some distance, in a yard of rust piles, and I told myself it was okay. We'd been noticed and it was okay. I was horrible to be there but it was okay. I shifted my weight from side to side, struggling to make the proper gestures, and told myself I was there for art, just as Emma was there for art. Two artists doing something specific. I dug my sketchbook from my bag. A prop, some proof of purpose.

Then another woman.

"This one is 82 and she is living alone, blind. Gave up hope for getting a house a long time ago. Before the quake she was working in a kindergarten where she had 45 children but now she has nothing and she doesn't know why she ended up in this situation. Says she just doesn't know why God doesn't let her die. You can hear the suffering in her voice. I mean can't you?"

I nodded yes. I must have heard the suffering in her voice. But it was all so impossibly distant.

"But when it's raining the sun will come out soon. And when it's dark it will be light soon."

--

Narine told me that after the earthquake the Soviets gave each family 10,000 rubles. But many families spent the money on elaborate memorials, because they needed to house the dead. The Soviets hastily built the *domiks*, promising the thousands of families they wouldn't live in them for longer than two years and placing their names on a waiting list for housing. And with the new *domiks*, with the new graves, the landscape changed. So even after the dust settled and the rubble got cleared from the roads, nobody really recognized Gyumri anymore. Many people left. And most of the families who stayed never rose to the top of the housing list. The apartments just didn't get built. Most remained in the *domiks* and the problems got denser and the roots of government corruption sunk deeper. The difference between having your number called, moving into an apartment and still being buried on the government's list—it's the difference between continuing with life and being buried with the dead. Even more people left. People have never stopped leaving.

--

Emma and I walked about a mile before spotting a taxi. As we rode, we stayed silent.

My thoughts went toward all the ways I didn't know how to be among what I found there. I didn't know at what angel to look at anything. And I hadn't given a lot of thought to this before arriving, no matter what Narine might have told me, what I'd read or watched on YouTube.

Experiencing Emma's quiet sent a wave of guilt rolling through me. And when I heard her sniffle in the front seat of the taxi, and for a moment believed she might be crying, a flicker of desire passed through me, to take my not-diminished parts, what was hunched in the backseat, and relinquish it over to her.

Then she said, "It was meant to be that we would find each other today. I mean this was *magical.*" And her voice was too buoyant for crying. I snapped back toward my indecisive feelings, where I didn't know what to think of her. But I agreed and said "It's magical, I know," and it came out sounding more automatic than intended. I tried mustering something interesting to add, a clever way of admitting my surprise at just how good a grasp she had on the place, but nothing came that didn't sound arrogant or self-deprecating, so I left the matter alone. I left it at just saying thank you for bringing me along, which she either didn't hear or ignored.

Outside of Levon's, Emma sprung up from the car to hug me, handing me a scrap of paper with her email address and phone number. I agreed to make plans to see her when I returned to Yerevan, before flying away for good, though inside I doubted I'd have that kind of energy.

--

I entered an empty house, a small miracle, and breathed easier in those large, Levon-free rooms. My body throbbed and ached, I felt a fresh stinging in my skin from sun. I considered getting into bed and staying hidden until morning. But I went to Levon's computer in the living room, something he'd welcomed me to do if I wanted, when I'd discovered that, though he had no wireless, he did have a dial-upped desktop. I pressed the space bar, bringing on the blue humming light, and fumbled through Russian Google, operating off of context and intuition as to what gray tab led to where, eventually finding my way to Gmail.

From Frannie. Subject: Hello?
Okay so I'm figuring you'll have email there… What the hell are you doing? You've scared the hell out of us! I went by the bakery looking for you, the woman there told me. She figured I knew. How did SHE know? Are you okay? How does this make any sense to you, do you know how –
I clicked back to my inbox.

From Eric. Subject: Feel better now?
First, let me just say I miss you.
Second, of all the places to go to relax and clear your head (if that's what you want to call it) in the world why would you choose there?
Your sister called and told me where you are.
You just left? Are you suicidal?

I'm giving serious consideration to coming over and finding you myself.

I've been doing some reading and you should read the cut and pasted information below.

Are you aware of the Armenia-Azerbaijan conflict—

I clicked off.

The sentences hit too real and not real at all. But people knew where I was. And to know they knew was enough. I shoved away any urge to respond, to apologize, justify, to explain. It occurred to me they had no idea why I had gone there. Would it make a difference to tell them I was there for art? Would it make a difference to me or to them? Would the justification do any good?

I retreated from my messages, from the computer, and retraced my steps through the dining room and down the stairs to the garden. I clicked off the house lights, hands careful on the rail as I descended the stairs, the day mostly gone from the sky. I sat on the bench, rubbing at my foot's healing blister and let the quiet wrap around me as I reflected on how much of an asshole I was.

Was I being an asshole for not giving in to my urge to respond? For not letting people know I was okay? A panicky bolt shot through me and I knew I had to answer my emails. And then I reminded myself I wasn't an asshole—not really, and to respond didn't have to be an admission of defeat. And the messages were some days old which meant it would look like I'd taken my time to respond. Like I'd exercised control, not seeing an immediate response as necessary. And in that way I'd won.

It hadn't taken them long to find out I was gone. Eric and Frannie's messages were stamped the day I'd arrived. I hadn't gotten far without someone noticing. And now I knew how long it would actually take for someone to discover my absence. It wasn't as long as I might of thought. I wasn't sure how I felt about that.

I lifted myself to return to the computer but the lights went on. Levon was back with heavy steps.

*Shit*, I thought.

"Come to hear my violin," he said from the top of the stairs.

I said, "Okay" with inflated enthusiasm. I said *okay* because *okay* was the best answer. Or, *okay* was the easiest answer. When Levon made suggestions, some elusive gnawing told me that anything other than compliance could prove a superfluous challenge.

Down in the basement, Levon pushed aside an ironing board covered in shirts, and pulled a wooden stool from the closet.

"Sit."

"Okay."

At the piano, with the violin nudged between chin and shoulder, his fat fingers banged the keys, twisted the violin pegs, worked to find the desired octaves. And when the violin was tuned, he stood and faced me with something new in his posture, something proud. He rattled out a long and phlegmy breath before swinging the bow harsh across the violin. He began to play a familiar tune.

"You know this, yes?" He swayed his broad body, flipping his head up and down like a horse.

"Yes," I squeaked out. I recognized it but couldn't place it. An off-noted sonata, something hanging sad in the air. "Mozart?"

Levon didn't answer. His question was not meant to incite conversation, making it all a little less uncomfortable. He closed his eyes and went toward music's muscle memory. I leaned in, elbow to my knee, conscious of looking the right degree of engaged, knowing he'd want this when he came back from where he'd gone. I clapped when the song ended and Levon sucked in a deep breath and began again, eyes still closed.

I sensed it could go on a while, but after the third song, Levon lifted his heavy lids and lumbered back to the piano seat. He flopped down, violin slumped between his legs, dwarfing the instrument still more. His shorts rode up and the pale flab of his upper thighs fanned over the bench. I clapped with what bit of enthusiasm I had on reserve. I whistled and stood, and Levon, head bent and sweating, raised his hand up nonchalantly as though to say what had just occurred was nothing. It was something between a salute and dismissive flick of the hand. He flashed me a coy smile.

"You like?"

"Yes. Very much. Thank you. Good night."

"Yes night."

For a moment, before I was totally turned to walk away, I thought of the gun and the rock and wondered if the time was right to say something. But I couldn't, wouldn't, all of it lodged too far down my throat.

He released me without challenges, so the thought of creating my own challenges seemed like a cruel way to go about the night.

--

Lying in bed, I felt around the inner recesses of my mind for the stories of the women at the *domiks*. Just the edges of stories, really. The hope-stripped fringes. What I'd seen slid by in tableaus. Caged pigeons behind my eyes, their guttural coo stuffed in my ears with fly swarms. A door chipped to pieces for heating. Old bread, impossible to eat. A woman, abducted and forced into marriage, only to be abandoned when the man moved to Russia for work. I lay on my stomach to feel the weight of my body press the tight spot in my abdomen against the bed, the knotty new scar. It bumped up and down, a blood-thumping. I pressed my face in the pillow and there were the children of *domiks* asleep in school dorms. A crowd of people ineligible for benefits and mistaken for not existing. A room with thin damp walls, piss buckets under chairs with the center cut out, tires stuffed in windows for insulation and clothing burned for heat, rabbits in cages in preparation for winter. I saw a canal behind a bus station, where the water rose through the floorboards of nearby rooms. I smelled it rotting between stones and under wood and rugs. I studied the colors. Ivory black, mixed gray. The color of a cut faucet and ice coating the floor. I watched for places to add mold to composites, raw umber, rats and wild dogs, large bags of wood, or anything else that might heat and melt the snow enough to drink.

Riding in the back of the taxi, on the way back from the precipice of others' tragic living, I'd buzzed in the back-seat about grants that might bring me back. But everything is different in the dark, laying pressed down in a bed alone. My artistic ambitions shriveled.

I hadn't Emma's capabilities to insert myself with such force into a scene. My objectives were rooted in a different place. I'd no compulsion to examine and display another's world for the sake of education or sharing. More than anything I'd come as a means of escaping where I was. And to create a self-portrait of sorts. A composition of my own making. Me against a new backdrop. But the more I was exposed to the traumas of Gyumri, that new backdrop, the less tidy and simple that composition became.

I held my face down in the pillow and asked myself how anyone ever sleeps?

--

Even though Eric rarely mentioned my art after that trip to NY, things stayed generally okay at first. We found a rhythm to things. And then maybe three months in, the real turn came. I'd gotten snowed in at his house. In his office, the cat scratched at the door to get in the room. The sky through the window was a hard gray. The remains of the blizzard were puffy and bright on the ground. So we dug in and I thought it couldn't be that bad. He had to finish a film-editing job, a sports commercial. An athletic blond girl, twirling a lacrosse stick, tossing a yellow ball in the air, leapt across the two massive computer monitors taking up most of his desk. Thumbnails of her ran along the bottom of the screens, each an isolated second of her motion. And something looking like Doppler radar, the seconds of her broke down into color, charted accordingly. It was at once boring and demanding of my attention. I managed after some time to thumb open a book taken from Eric's bookshelf.

Other than New York, we'd never spent more than twenty-four hours together and usually far less than that. Eric, prone to disappearing into his work, could go for days without leaving the house. It never bothered me. The intermittent distance felt just fine. Helpful in fact. Too much time together made us vulnerable to small but annoying arguments, misfires in our communication, conflicts that never seemed to have a definitive start.

I looked up and Eric wasn't working any more. He was on Facebook, and I could hear the message blips. I could see the thread of text running along the side of the two screens. And the thumbnail face, a young, pale woman with a flapper haircut whom I didn't recognize. Several emoji of hearts appeared on the screen. And so I asked.

His exasperated explanation was centered on why I should feel guilty for asking about it at all. It was only a kind woman who lived in England, who made him feel good about himself. A friend he'd met online who understood how hard he was on himself, how hard he worked.

He stopped talking, studied the skepticism on my face and reached for my hand, trying another approach.

"But we spoke about you, too. She saw your picture and she thinks you're pretty."

"That should make me feel good?" I retracted my hand.

And then he demanded I leave the room.

"If you can't leave you need to at least exit the fucking room. I've got work and you're being inconsiderate.'"

I sat on the couch next to the cat and watched *In Bruges*. I'd almost gotten to the credits before he came out of the office. He stomped into the kitchen and took an arm-full of Sapporo beer cans from the refrigerator.

"You're still here?"

I didn't answer, stayed still, kept my numb expression and waited for the moment to pass, waited for him to disappear back into his office.

I fell asleep on the couch. At some point after that he woke me with a hand through my hair.

"Sorry," he whispered with beer breath. "Let's get out of the house."

It was 3 a.m.

He had one of those terribly large trucks that could drive over anything. He did sharp donuts in the shopping center parking lot and I gripped the seat next to him, laughing to muffle my fear. I thought we would die, and I thought it wouldn't have been worth it.

# 6

I woke and realized the gun and rock no longer sat on the chest and a panic thumped through me. I scanned the room, wondering if I'd moved it myself. I decided to wait in the room until Levon left for work. I had to pee. I found a water bottle, placed a towel on the floor and hunched over it, then climbed back under the heavy blankets and considered ways to disappear, ways to invert, discover new depths of myself, unexplored space that might serve to shelter me. I envisioned myself spanning the deep until the other side opened. Some endless spot of otherness I could claim as myself. Some piece of me light years from disasters, large or small. But I saw none of that. I only lay there. A small and present, solid but crack-prone mass.

I fell back into a half-sleep and had a lucid dream of children helping their parents chop tree trunks into chunks. The children held miniature axes and wore large, clear plastic bags, their faces poking out of face-sized holes. They watched as I passed.

Then a light knocking on my door. The clock said 10:28. I peeked out to find Melik.

"I am so sorry," I said.

He wore a new expression. A cool kind of embarrassment, or maybe pity for how damaged I must have looked.

What could be a sadder sight than an insomniac startled out of shallow sleep?

"Oh no it's fine, I'm sorry. Do you want to—"

"Yes. Definitely."

"Oh okay. You can… Just come get me when you're ready."

--

I decided to write Frannie an elaborate email, but by the time I navigated Russia's internet and made my way to Gmail, I was met with the white text box and a vacuous mind in dire need of coffee.

Subject: hi.

I'm fine here and having a great time painting! Glad you touched base with Narine. She's great! Please tell Eric to calm the fuck down. More soon! Love, Sara.

I hated my decision to end with *love*. But I hit send with no revision. She would see right through the saccharine word and all those exclamation marks. Had I ever written that to her? *Love.* When had I last said it? Had I ever?

Love her I did, but that love lacked the muscle to push through the mud of residual emotion that came from living around each other for so long and in such different ways.

This was nothing to love: how she was too young to know our father so the first man in her life was our mother's chubby boyfriend. Charlie, a car mechanic who always filled our apartment with the smell of oil. Oil always saturating his clothes and streaking up his arms. Always leaving the scum of it in the bathroom sink. Always shitting in our toilet. Always with Charlie, our mother's chubby boyfriend, the smell of oil and shit in our apartment.

It was nothing to love. Charlie hung out at our apartment as though he lived there and he didn't. He'd show up at unpredictable times, unannounced in the afternoon, after school when our mother wasn't home. My sister took to sitting on his lap and eating the spaghetti he made. On weekends there were trips to the shopping mall or Hershey Park and my mother in the sunlight, off the couch, smelling cleaner and quicker to smile and laugh. Charlie stopped knocking and took to just entering the house and my sister would squeal with happiness each time. How ill it made me to watch her look up at him. To watch her give him a towel when he wiped his oily hands in the shit-smelling bathroom. She was not put off by Charlie's smells or his dirt. And so when he moved in, when he married my mother, something within Frannie settled into completion.

An earth-bound man who wore oil out of the ground. Nothing like our flying father who was made of inhuman speed and crisp uniforms.

I allowed myself to believe Frannie was lucky I emailed her at all. And I allowed myself to feel put out by the task.

--

I told myself to brush home away and to forget about the rock and the gun, at least for the time being. It was time to dig in and deflect. My easel and supplies laid out, Melik positioned in the field some 15 feet away, I returned to recording some small patch of the world, I returned to a more comfortable surface, before the sun moved too far beyond the shell of the buildings and I lost the horizon completely.

I reminded Melik to keep his back turned. He complied, in his black and white striped shirt, on Naples Yellow grass, one leg up and one leg down. I wondered if for him it was only marginally tolerable, or if it represented respite from something. Perhaps I was saving him from somewhere, or perhaps I was keeping him hostage. I didn't ask.

Occasionally I heard him speak. The words got jumbled in the wind and never reached me intact.

"Just talk louder," I yelled.

--

I asked, "Why do you call it Ghost Town, anyway? Do people say they see ghosts here?"

"Well, what do you think? You could say ghostliness, more so than ghosts."

--

Melik asked, "This thing you call a little man. Was it toxic?"

I told him it depended on his definition of toxic.

"But you are okay. You are still here and breathing?"

"It didn't take my breathing. And not all of my hereness."

--

Melik said, "Tell me something you are sorry to be embarrassed you were wrong about."

"I don't know."

"Why?"

"What?"

"Okay."

"For a significant portion of my life I thought the phrase *for all intents and purposes* was *for all intensive purposes.*"

--

Melik said, "I don't believe that anything can ever be completely nailed down and grounded. But painting seems to do something close to this for you?"

"Yeah."

"Taking things and trying to freeze them in place as you've said?"

"Exactly."

"Well, I don't know about exactly. I mean actually no, maybe I don't agree."

"Then tell me why I paint?"

"No actually I don't believe you like to freeze things. You want to fill a void. To complete yourself. Or to try to, I mean. That's anyone of us. But you're not trying to freeze anything in place. In fact, quite the opposite."

"Okay. Maybe I'm just happy to decipher variations in light. Maybe I don't need everything."

"Definitely not exactly that."

--

I asked, "When do you think Levon sleeps?"

"Sleeps? You would know better than me."

"Thanks."

--

Melik asked, "What does sadness feel like to you?"

"A ping. You know the kind I mean?"

--

Melik asked, "What do you like about it here?"

"How slow it is."

"Now *that's* funny."

--

Melik asked, "So what do you see? Whatever it is you examine, record, do you actually believe it to be true?"

"Maybe it only matters if I like what I find."

--

I asked, "Are you awake?"
"Mostly."

--

Tightening the stripes in Melik's shirt pulled out the violet of his shoulders and settled the ochre and white into place. I'd pushed his torso up from the ground. Him in his world, with blood under his skin, and me making something two-dimensional from it. I almost felt I'd accomplished something.

--

We lay on the grass sliding toward our separate kinds of sleep. Me, to a familiar and dreamless, shallow state. Melik to a deeper place, or so it seemed, given his steady, rhythmic breathing. Eventually, a dull ache in my legs and the crook of my neck said I'd laid there too long. I may have slept, but if so it was that sleep where you can't be sure it happened. My eyes opened to a different sky, a twirling ultramarine of day's end. I bent my knees, one at a time, the pressure a proof of my body's limits, and turned to the moist breathing of another human. Melik on his back, snoring, hat on chest. I thought of Eric and how I'd liked to have seen his reaction to the scene. I'd have liked to witness his dispirited face. And it worried me that I might call him when I got back. The whole chain of thoughts wrapped something hollow and ominous around me. The same ominousness that came when I thought of the rock and the gun, the same bleak that comes with the residual effects of mistakes.

--

I asked Melik about his memory of the earthquake and immediately regretted it. If I was going to get personal I should have asked about his wife, or France. But I knew I didn't because I wanted to keep him defined as a person who belonged where I found him. Someone who fit into the quiet landscape of broken buildings and yellow fields. To learn of the happiness and promise that awaited him in France would have broken him out of the composition, exposed me to a dimension I wasn't prepared to consider, an added expanse in the natural divide of our worlds. But somehow, the earthquake, that tragic crumbling, still crumbling all around us— that felt okay.

"You must have been pretty young, right?"

Melik kept his usual ease, letting the long stalk of grass fall from his mouth as he began to talk, a sleepiness still in his throat. "Well, sure. I must premise it with the fact that it's something between true memory and a fiction. I mean I was only two years old."

I nodded, as though to say of course, I'd expected as much, even though in reality, I'd thought he was much older.

"For example," he said. "I've got a fog of visuals. Like gravestones. The road lined with crosses and coffins. Black and red coffins along the streets, stacked five high. People peeking under sheets to see what bodies could be recognized. The mud holes dug, and the burials, the ceremonies and just that sound of grief. Like, old women crying. Men yelling to each other, and my neighbor. She was pregnant and worried that something would be wrong with the baby. She thought it would come out with its brain cracked. My sister, she's older. Growing up she always would draw pictures of broken houses, crosses and Xs for eyes on faces in red and black crayons."

He laid back down on the grass. I sensed he was reliving his grief and I'd beckoned it there. An elastic sensation of earth-hued sadness joined us and threatened to get out of hand. So I sprung up to the easel, picked the canvas up and hovered it over him. He accepted the shift in the scene, took the cue, squinted up and said with the cooing encouragement normally reserved for children or pets or idiots, "Very nice. I think it will be done soon. Yes?"

"Done soon? Don't know. But we've frozen some time there."

--

Levon at the computer playing solitaire, called my name, prompted me toward the living room couch and gestured for me to sit.

"Okay."

It had to be about the rock and gun, I knew, so I curled my hands in my lap and said, "I am so sorry, Levon. I'm sorry and I had no right."

Levon went motionless, a vacancy in his face I'd come to know as him not understanding me. He leaned in and handed over a basket of plums from the coffee table, then stood and crossed the room, opening the cabinet under the television, pulling out a thick book, a photo album, its vinyl cover adorned with light blue bells and roses.

"Here books maybe you like."

He placed the album in my lap, lowered himself into the chair beside me, lit a cigarette and cleared his throat before inhaling and locking in on the television. An attractive and heavily made up woman interviewed what was probably a ce-lebrity, gauging by his severe hairstyle, the crisp jeans and suede vest. They sat in a white walled studio on what looked like white lawn chairs, a white porcelain tea set between them on a small white table.

I opened the album, pictures spilling out, the chewed and yellowed pages crackling as I pried them apart. Maybe because of the sound of the pages or the pictures slipping, but Levon snapped back to, suddenly back and stamping out his cigarette, a hand out for the album. The gesture said, *I will not let you break anything else in this house.* He balanced the album over his large bare knees.

"Now I tell you who." He pointed to a photo. "Sister."

In a frayed, black and white photo a boy sat in a wagon. A girl stood nearby. Both looked into the camera with tight-lipped smiles. I didn't ask if it was the sister he liked and died or one of the two still living, but I concluded by the careful way he said the word *sister* that he liked her and she'd died.

He lit another cigarette, the smoke constricting the room.

He pointed to another picture. "This is Nagorno-Kara-bakh."

It was Levon, with what must have been his wife, son and daughter, standing in front of a large sculpture of a man and a woman chiseled out of pink volcanic stone. I recognized the monument from photos of the region I'd seen online. The man and woman, half immersed in a mound of earth, was a revered symbol of Armenian heritage. Levon and his family stood beside the hill, some distance from the mound and the statue. Levon was smiling. He looked happy to be there. The face of the son and the daughter looked bright enough, alive, albeit vaguely bored, but the wife was all sadness.

I asked, "When? What year?"

He stamped out the cigarette, a quarter finished. "Two years."

"My work," he said, moving to another photo. A woman with gray streaked hair, sitting next to him at a foldout table, in an office room. They held up water bottles like champagne glasses.

Another photo. "Me in army. Germany. 1986." It was a thinner, smiling Levon, wearing army greens, holding a gun just like the one from the guestroom.

"Hey, my dad was in the military, too."

I identified the squint in Levon's eyes as him trying to untangle the meaning of my words. I moved on.

"You look happy," I said.

"Rotary club," he grumbled, pointing to a photo of men lounging on a picnic blanket.

"Oh wow."

Rotary Club was the last photograph. Levon closed the album, placed it next to his feet and strayed back to the television.

I sat thinking of what to say or do next. I sat thinking that if I were to ask Levon where his family was, it would have been then. And maybe that was how he invited it. I picked up a plum and rolled it between my palms, and after a few heavy seconds, decided to ask no questions. I stood up, believing I'd gone to the far reaches of our connection, I'd gone there and for some seconds I lingered, and then I said good night, straining to put some pep in the words.

# 7

My face in the morning, round and pink in the bathroom mirror, sunburn peeling from my nose in slivers. I'd developed creases along my mouth from dry air. The shower was still cold. Which, despite the heat, never felt like relief. I hadn't figured out the water heater and told myself it was too late, would be too embarrassing at that point, to ask my host for instruction on something so basic. I took my morning birdbath in the sink, splashed upward oval strokes between my legs, over my torso and shoulders. But it was time to wash the dust and cigarette smoke from my hair, so I angled the crown of my head under the tub faucet, swearing under my breath as the cold water fell over me.

Upstairs, Levon in the kitchen, the coffee and the bread. He was still in his red tracksuit and sandals and it occurred to me it must be Saturday. I sat down across from him at the kitchenette.

"Melik not coming today," he said.

"No Melik today?"

"No Melik today."

I swallowed back resentment and it knotted in my throat. He should have told me, I thought.

Levon rose from his seat. "Come see French room upstairs." He pointed to the ceiling with his cigarette.

I cleared my throat, shook my head no and pointed to my watch and the easel I'd sat in the corner of the room. He raised his coffee cup and took the last swig, then slapped the cup down and made an uncharacteristically energetic gesture with his arm, as though to say, *Oh come on, you only live once.* Or, *You can spare a few goddamn minutes.* I wanted a gesture that would say, *But you know how terribly awkward it gets when we're alone together.* But I didn't have a clue how to pull that off.

In the French room upstairs, the top floor of Levon's house, free summer classes were offered for children who wanted to learn French. This is as much as I could figure out. The room spanned the house. It smelled of paint and sun flooded in through the large, bare windows. The room felt new and hardly touched, despite all the signs of it being a classroom. The French and Armenian Flags hung from the wall, book-ending a podium. Three long tables ran the length of the room. Crayon depictions of France hung haphazardly from wall tacks. Eiffel Towers of various sizes and colors, beret-wearing stick figures and flags. Levon pointed to a framed poster of Mount Ararat. "Come see," he said. "Ark. There."

"Noah's Ark?"

"Yes."

Levon's finger traced the spot of Noah's Ark. A crescent shape visible from under the snow. It could have been anything jutting up, but it certainly looked like an ark.

"Nice, wow." I waved my hand around the room. "The whole thing. Wow."

"And Rotary Club funny." Levon crossed the room and stood in front of a framed illustration of a teddy bear wearing a red tracksuit and playing a violin.

"You!"

"Yes!"

"Nice."

"You speak French""

"No, you?"

"No. Teachers."

"Oh."

I sifted through some booklets on the table. French-Armenian phrase books and blank compositions. I considered if it was a good time to mention the gun and the rock, thinking I could just say, *I had no business touching it and I'll certainly pay for the damages.* But he didn't bring it up and I didn't know how to begin. The subject of the rock and gun were getting further and further away, off where the request to understand how to work the water heater lived, where things that I couldn't broach went to fester, just out of reach.

Levon walked over to the window and lit a cigarette.

"Levon, I should go."

He stamped the cigarette out on the floor, said something Armenian under his breath. "You go," he said.

--

Music was coming from the other side of Melik's door, maybe the Beatles. I paused and thought about knocking, but moved on before the urge kicked in. With that knot of resentment vibrating up my throat, threatening to burst out, I walked fast, hoping to shake it off.

In the field, I considered ways to smooth the half figure, the missing subject, into the canvas' landscape. I could smudge him out completely. I could leave him unshaped, unconnected. His color wasn't worked out, the figure was wrong, the ornament of him was lost. But I decided to wait and see if he'd return the next day.

I sat in the field, wanting to charge toward the building shells, but decided to jog in a circle until my leg cramped.

I returned to my easel. An hour passed, then two. I'd hardly been there long enough, but still.

The minutes smothered me with a blanket of forever.

--

The photo of the building on the wall in the bakery had said to me: *It's okay if things don't feel finished. They can still be valuable.*

I loved this most about the photo.

But the photo could not win out in that field, in that silence. And that petrified me. The photo had brought me to a day that had turned into a gaping hole. I stood at the edge and I floundered.

I walked away from the easel, away from Melik's partial figure, and lay in the field, my arms up over my eyes to block the sun. I saw Narine behind the counter, smoothing her apron. And I saw me in those idle days after my surgery, leading up to Armenia, my insides throbbing as they worked to heal themselves, the intermittent stab with the wrong motion of my torso.

I lay there and felt no pain, no stabs, no throbs. Only the ever-present buzz in my head.

--

Instead of taking my easel and supplies in the house, I leaned them against the courtyard fence and tiptoed away. I didn't want to stir Levon. What I wanted was to walk with no real agenda, so I pointed myself in the general direction of Vartanants Square, deciding to brave a new road, cutting a hard left, challenging myself.

I took a side street and stopped at a small, near-empty amusement park. A winding slate path lined with thirsty trees and a series of precarious metal rides—a clanking carousel and squeaking swing—all painted in bright primaries. I sat on a bench in front of small cars moving slowly up and around in a counter clock-wise motion. A single child was on the ride. He banged the metal sides of the car, bounced around, either bored or over stimulated. He was autistic or developmentally delayed in some way, going by the grunts and the repetitive motions he made with a slightly curled, left hand. The child's mother sat on a nearby bench, knitting. She shot me a look that said, *why would you be here with no child? And, furthermore, why would you choose to sit in the presence of my child?* I thought to take out my sketchbook but changed my mind, knowing that drawing would root myself to the moment in a way I probably wasn't up for. A drawing of this park, a drawing of these park rides, a drawing of this park's lone child and mother. Even if the urge found me, somehow capturing this disabled child's quick and jerky gestures, and the mother's casual air, made it all the more uncomfortable. I got up and moved on before I had to witness the child falling from the car.

In that moment there was nothing interesting to me about trying to capture a child on paper or even a child's park, other than maybe that particular one's strange, curled hand. I decided to take this as further affirmation that I'd no inherent tug toward having children. I walked from the park with a lightness I hadn't expected.

--

I hadn't thought it out when I invited it—what might happen if Melik wasn't around to see the work through. To invite a human figure into the canvas meant inviting chaos to the process. I could only blame myself.

It's an investment to draw a living being.

I thought of Melik as I walked and returned to blaming myself for inviting him in. I had chosen to paint him, perhaps carelessly. His sudden lack of availability left my day uprooted. It reminded me of the mutual responsibility the task took. The best subjects were inanimate objects. I'd always thought that. Objects can't question or quit.

--

I'd clung to the idea that one must draw hands well to draw the figure at all. The revelation had presented itself in a *how to draw* workbook found in a stack of magazines when we'd been packing to move east. *Hands are a hard task to master*, the book said. *The most difficult part of the body to capture.* The workbook called it *an articulate organ.* What the phrase meant exactly I could not say at that age but I knew it held authority. *It's difficult to know where to start with the hands*, the book admitted. *It's difficult to break the hand down into a simple, digestible structure. It's easy to want to see it all as straight lines instead of complex arches.*

I don't recall my father ever drawing hands. He was more about oversized cartoonish mittens and hands shoved in cartoonish pockets, techniques the book would tell me were *tactics for dodging the challenge.*

Because of the white-out of my grief, I remember little of the day our mother decided to tell Frannie and I our father had died. But I remember it was the day I decided to master drawing the hand.

She told us in a Denny's restaurant. First, we all ordered moons over my hammy at our mother's insistence, because that was our father's favorite. Frannie wanted waffles and instead of denying or capitulating, my mother ordered the waffles along with the moons over my hammy. Then she told us as the waitress walked away with the menus. She told us with me sitting across the booth and my sister sitting on her lap. Smoothing back my sister's wild curls, she said he wasn't coming back because something happened to his brain.

The rest is a matter of fleeting movements, what hints could get through the blankness of feeling. I think I cried first and I think Frannie followed, which made our mother cry. I know we left before our food came, our mother swooped us up before it got too embarrassing. We would have walked back because we had no car, but that walk is lost.

Back in my uncle's basement apartment, I locked myself in the bathroom and took to drawing hands on the wall with a pencil. My mother eventually gave up banging on the door, or so she must have, because I was in there all night. I know it was all night because I woke up in the bathtub, sun leaking through the small window above the toilet. When I eventually unlocked the door, my mother was standing there with a red, wet face and hard, narrow eyes. That face of hers was a clear moment. She looked at the walls, the faint pencil sketches of gestural hands, and said it would be a long time before I could be trusted again. She said it with little breath, in a small and strained voice, as though from the top of a hole. Those pencil hands stayed on the wall for the rest of the time we lived in my uncle's basement.

We'd move into an apartment eventually and some sem-blance of normalcy crept in slow like a moss all through the box rooms and cream renter's carpet, on that generic deck that overlooked the generic decks of others across the parking lot. *A nice apartment*, my mother said the day we arrived.

She got a job and started to smell different. Some sort of spicy musk replaced the whiskey most days of the week. She got a car. A *nice car*, she called it. A minivan of some bland color she proudly declared as cappuccino. A *nice color*, she argued when I called it boring. She made a *nice* world for us and I hated how *nice* it was because none of it was supposed to be.

--

I went where I knew to go, toward the Russian restaurant and found Melik sitting outside with a man whose nose looked broken several times over. He sprang up when he noticed me, asked, "Are you better?" He hugged me, smelled boozy.

"Better?"

He stepped back and studied my face. "This morning Levon said you were sick."

"Sick?"

"Sick." Melik pulled out a chair for me.

"I'm fine."

"Good. Nice you are out. Meet my friend Aram. He's a painter, too." He tossed his head toward the broken nosed man and said with a rare brightness to his words, "You two are painters!"

Aram offered a subtle nod and I tried to synch up our reactions, matching his aloof expression by keeping my face muscles slack.

"There was an American here earlier, too," Aram said smirking, shifting in his seat. "I think he was American. Looked and sounded so, at least. Ah. Two whole Americans in Gyumri. Invasion!"

Melik grabbed an unused water glass from the next table and poured me a vodka. They were drunk. I could tell by the table, a mess with cigarette ash and dribbles of vodka, marks of a long, sloppy afternoon. I said how glad I was for the company, letting out a sigh and slumping deep in the chair. I took a long sip, an illustration of my ease and gratitude, the cool vodka running a slow burn through my chest. Aram kept a smug gaze locked on me and I pretended not to notice, I pretended I was used to casually drinking straight vodka under the hot sun.

Aram was arrogant, I decided, but still I was glad Melik had a friend, even if knowing as much altered my understanding of him. He'd never spoken of friends, painter friends or otherwise friends. And with friends, Melik was suddenly more grounded in Gyumri. The inevitable shift in our relationship, the gap between us, widened with this knowledge. Melik with friends was a reminder I didn't know him all that well. He was home. I'd be gone soon, eventually forgotten by the few people I'd met. He would stay as long as he wanted or needed and when he left people would cry and maybe try to talk him out of going or at least throw him a party. I was on a tourist visa. It's amazing our paths had crossed at all, and it brought about a fleeting ping of sadness.

Melik's phone rang and he jerked up from the table, wandered down the sidewalk, leaving Aram and I to stare past each other in silence. I wondered if it was his wife or yet another friend and the sad ping passed back through. Aram tapped an unlit Camel against the table and was the first to break the silence. "May I ask you? Do you think of art as therapy?" He spoke in the same perfect English as Melik, but he was jittery, lacked his friend's taciturn manners. I said yes I did think of art as therapy, and wondered if Melik had mentioned the specifics of my work. Maybe he'd been bitching about the portrait. Not knowing what words might have been used to define my work—to define me—was a cruelty.

Aram rolled his eyes back into his head, raised his voice, "Motivation, the need for therapy. Or, no. Okay, so not necessarily the word *motivation*, maybe the word *obligation* sounds better for English. What do you think?"

I worked to take apart the threads, searching for the question in the words. "Do you mean you want to know what motivates me?"

He darted his eyes toward the sky, and looked as though he was heading to some dark and well-tread corner of his psyche. After a heavy pause, he snapped his fingers. "Let me describe my practice to you."

"Okay."

"Okay. After the earthquake, with the loss of my father, I lost my faith. So, I began to make constructions inside my head. My head was this vessel for grief. You see it was empty so I decided I should put something back in it. Okay. So, when I say *obligation* I guess I mean that obligation includes life's question of how to properly exercise memory. How to tell a disaster's story? And from there, other questions, such as the necessary big questions of what to do and how to do it? You see, I self-diagnosed myself with *container syndrome*. It is a phrase I created describing what gets caged in the head." He poked his head with the unlit Camel, then lit it. "Symptoms include a need to tell stories as a means of dumping something and the something never fully getting dumped."

Aram paused to inhale the cigarette and examined it in his hand. I nodded, not clear if this was the best way to react. He had chosen a swift course for our conversation and I sensed that how I joined did not matter. I could sit dumbly and just go along for the ride. And maybe that's what I should do, I thought, because he seemed a guy to handle with kid gloves. Fragile, off-keel. Whereas I might normally be inclined to roll my eyes at someone speaking as he did, his explanation of practice was not your typical patronizing. Some volatility seemed bubbling right below the surface.

Melik returned to his seat and Aram continued, "The whole of the body is a vessel for grief, but mostly the head holds the weight. Trickling down and circulating out from this point." Aram stood and pushed his chair away, lifted his arms up in a stigmata pose and rolled his neck around. "*This* point. The trick is to compose something with it. To command the circulation's direction and rhythm. The beauty of grief lives in the fact that no two griefs look or ache alike. It can hemorrhage out from no place other than the artist. Grief is dumbly loyal to its birthplace and loyal to its canvas. So, for example, my grief isn't engineered from the place of dreams, either. Just the temperamental, sharp edges of real, past and now. It wouldn't know how to start otherwise. It wouldn't know where to go, how to circulate."

Aram cut his monologue and knelt down to meet me eye-level. "The canvas is safe," he whispered. "It's a waiting space. And the grief can run free there, safely along the length of the room, along the length of the years."

I nodded approval and thought about what to say. I gauged Melik's relaxed face and determined this was likely Aram's usual mode. Maybe I should have commented on Aram's description of grief, the poetry of it, a simple compliment maybe, but I decided my continued nodding and smiling would do. Regardless of whether his speech was intended for me, based on what Melik might have told him, or if this was just how he always talked, I decided my response was not needed. I swigged down more vodka and tried to look pensive, as though I was pondering his words. In my head I was trying to think of how I might respond if I were back home, if this were a friend, but I couldn't pinpoint what that might look like. I was without my everyday gestures and ways. They'd all been switched out by new modes of reacting and strategies for keeping composure. Gyumri required new tactics, new expression, and I was just beginning to fully know the extent of it.

Aram rose from his knees, outstretched his arms again. "Excuse me but I must go take my son to soccer practice."

--

Melik and I needed water and food but Melik suggested we find it elsewhere, so we headed down Sargsyan Street. Some stray kids kicked a soccer ball back and forth over a rusted car propped up over an old refrigerator. As we passed the kids scattered, yelling in a way I took as frantic. They may have been angry or joking but regardless I liked seeing the rare burst of life on a Gyumri street.

I asked Melik, "Levon told you I was sick?"

"Yes."

"Why?"

"I don't know. Because you were sick."

"I wasn't."

"Sorry about Aram. I hope it was not too much for you." Something hollow in Melik's tone told me he meant what he said, he wasn't just trying to change the topic.

"Too much for me? No. But tell me more about him." It's not like me to probe, but asking about Aram felt almost necessary.

"Aram?" Melik adjusted his hat and stayed silent for a minute, perhaps searching out the best words. "Well, Aram has never left Armenia, has lived in Gyumri all his life. He lives in an apartment near the edge of town. His household includes three generations of family, which as you know is not so unusual for us. So, Aram spends most days in his apartment building's attic studio, when he is not working. He trained in art and works as an art therapist. In school he was not taken seriously, I think. He and his work were considered too emotional. So maybe that has made him even more emotional. But he has a son and a daughter and I think he's probably a good father."

After some silence I said, "I get Aram." But I was half-lying. I wasn't convinced I got him at all, but I needed to kill that weighty Gyumri quiet with something. More accurate would have been to say I'd found him interesting. More accurate would be to say, I lost my father, too. But mentioning my own father would shift the moment completely. And it was not a moment that fit in the chain of moments. Not in that quiet. Not in that heavy air.

I pushed on, despite making the wrong point. Or, if not the wrong point, a point with no true shape. Because there was all that vodka in me and because I needed to keep that quiet away. "I get what he says about container syndrome. It's a good way to describe the dark in one's head. I mean this pressure builds up in your head and then you realize, *bam*. There is the light. And then a weightlessness that follows when you're caged in your head with realizations. Realizations like you are just another person and there is no universal suffering and you are so fucking small and that's actually okay. That it's good, actually. Reassuring. What is the good that comes out of it? The good comes in how resilient you are? How you can make art out of it, I guess. Or writing. How you break through? Jumping out, somewhere new. That."

I was drunk and not sure what sense I was making or if Melik was even listening so I stopped. He lifted his face toward me for a moment and smiled a tired smile. A smile that said he was humoring me. Maybe I should have just explained I knew what it was like to lose a parent.

I needed water and food. I needed to not be drunk. I needed my headache to go away. I shut up and retreated to the obvious truth rolling around in my head: I could never understand Aram, dead father or not.

I imagined him with his kids. The sight of him driving his son to soccer practice. Him sticking his head out his apartment window, his kids playing below. The sight of his playing kids, helping to lure him from his head-cage and for however long that lasts, if only for a fleeting few moments in a day, him not feeling so damaged, not so unsettled in his body. Him feeling complete. Just simple and clear and as undamaged as the children below the window, flickering lightly through the dust.

I felt these scenes as a soreness in my gut. Not the soreness I'd known from surgery, but the soreness of envy. Not over Aram's imagined children, but rather the symbol they stood for—something grounding, some completion.

The heat of the day rose through my body with the vodka. I cut through the silence, continued the word-mess I'd started.

"You know what I can't stand, Melik?"

"What?"

"The idea that family is viewed as how we legitimize our place in the world."

"What does that have to do with anything?"

"You said Aram is a good father. As though this was a way of justifying everything else he is. To say that he is a good father negating all other issues he might have."

"What?"

"No you did. That is how you described it. You could say Sara is a really good—

*whatever*, but that wouldn't negate any sort of anything or whatever else about me."

Melik shot me a face that told me to quite while there was still hope to not foil the evening and I did as his face suggested.

Envy is a cruel visitor.

We walked through the dusk, I hovered around the dark heavy spots in my gut. I thought: *I've brought too much here with me.*

--

We came to a café. An unexpected shift in the landscape. Modern and out of place, brass-trimmed, nearly all glass, metal and mirrors. Blue gel lights hung above a floor of orange couches and everything shined. It lightened me some.

At the counter we ordered sandwiches and bottles of water. We slouched into a couch and a waitress with cat-like features delivered our order in a silent flutter. A band played in a corner of the room—five teenaged, slight-framed boys. The singer, a bleach blond streak of hair winged over his eye, sung with a low mumbling, baritone voice into a staticy mic. I could make out the words of John Lennon's *Imagine*.

"Not confident in his English," said Melik, through a yawn, wiping his mouth and stretching out his legs.

The band transitioned into the Doors' *When You're a Stranger* and the singer's voice gained a stilted bounce. At a corner table near the stage, two girls and a boy, synched their pronounced jerks to each staticy, bouncy lyric. Sitting arrow straight and drab-faced on a couch to the side, what were likely the band's sisters and mothers. They were the café's only other patrons besides us. A limp kind of energy waved through the room.

I asked Melik to tell me about his writing progress and he snapped to, as if remembering where he was or what he was doing, widening his eyes and re-stretching his legs.

"Stuck in a dream scene," he said. His body limped again.

I decided not to ask him to elaborate, knowing he'd tell me if he wanted me to know.

The band stopped and the cafe gave into a timid clapping to which the singer responded by mumbling something into the mic and slipping off stage. The rest of the band shrugged off their instruments and followed. The corner table of teenagers followed, too. As they passed our couch Melik called out to them, stopping them in their tracks. They brightened up, and the singer's posture flinched straight for a moment. He said something back to Melik and they all laughed harder.

"They are The Pillows," one of their friends chimed up in English, making the rest of them halt their laughs. "We say pillow because you can go sad or go happy. Always need your pillow. Both for crying and laughing. The pillow is always."

"Nice," I said.

After some back and forth with Melik, they slinked out of the café in a more reserved mass with heads re-drooped. Outside, they were no longer musicians and groupies, they were kids collected in a parking lot, sitting on the curb, lighting cigarettes.

"Gyumri nights need this kind of youth," Melik mumbled. "They will all move to Yerevan soon. Or further."

"Did they say that?"

"No. It just is."

The mothers and sisters remained on their couch, unanimated, occasionally passing words between each other, some of them with vacant stares pointed at the now empty stage, some of them with eyes on the kids through the window. All of them wore something like malaise or fatigue, near palpable.

Melik cleared his throat, "I am wondering what to do now."

"Tonight?"

"No. Everything. Marriage."

"Oh."

"I'm afraid she doesn't love me. Maybe I'm afraid she will love me and want kids. Not sure what is right."

"You're afraid to go back? Are you afraid to have kids?"

"Are you?"

"Afraid to go back? Sure, kind of. The truth is, I didn't tell anyone I was coming here so they're all pretty pissed now that they know. But I won't have kids. I mean, I can't have kids."

"Of course you can have kids."

"No actually I *can't*. I mean it's okay. Really I don't mind. But I think maybe I'm a little worried about when I'm older. Worrying that I will be sad it didn't happen, you know? Probably all due to some overwhelming loneliness that will just come over me one day. The bio-clock. Some fear of dying alone, maybe mixed with some primal tug to just procreate for the sake of humans in general. That would suck, but it's not uncommon."

"It doesn't have to be the thing that makes your life great," he whispered, watching the boy band out the window, blank-faced.

"The thing is I don't really like kids. Actually, it's something I have only admitted out loud quite recently. The not wanting kids, I mean. It's because of the tumor. It's funny but when they told me I don't think it really sunk in. The first thing I thought was, will I miss it? The tumor, the little man? Will I feel the absence? And I feel it sometimes, like a phantom limb. I wonder if I'll always divide my life between before and after. Pre little man and post little man. If I will end up just burying it quietly, never speaking about it, or pulling it out as a party anecdote from time to time. It's just wild that I feel it sometimes. And I wonder if that's what being pregnant feels like."

"Wait. Did you say you didn't tell anyone you would come here?"

"Yes. I mean they figured it out. It's fine."

"Why?" He leaned toward me, a look that told me I should feel ashamed.

I laughed. "I don't know. I wanted this to be a private experience."

"Jesus."

Melik studied my face for a few long seconds before turning back to watch through the window. "When this is behind us, do you think whatever we are returning to will be different? I mean, I want it to be so different that I have a hard time remembering what it was like to begin with. Some days I think I wouldn't know my direction back to France if I tried. But I don't know if that's true or just wishful thinking."

"Do you want to stay here?"

"Fuck no."

"Will you help me with the painting tomorrow?"

"Yes of course. We'll take as long as you need."

"I broke the rock off the top of the gun in Levon's guestroom."

Melik laughed. I laughed, too. A good sound for as long as it lasted.

But it didn't last long, because there he was, walking past the boy band and through the glass doors. There he was under blue gel lights in Gyumri: Eric. Walking to the counter, greeted by the cat-like waitress.

I slinked low and asked Melik for his hat, then hopped to the adjacent couch, keeping my back to the counter. I was taken by my own reflexes, how quick I moved, like a feral animal in fear of being captured.

"What's wrong?" Melik laughed.

I searched out words and eventually they came out thin and small.

"Someone I know. The counter. Tall guy."

Melik furled his eyebrows and studied the counter. "The American, yeah Aram and I saw him earlier. You met him?" He matched my whisper.

"No, I *know* him. I mean, he's... okay tell me what he's doing. I need to get out of here. Whatever happens I can't let him see me. Please. What's he doing right now? Is he looking over?"

"Okay okay. Well he's over by the counter."

"Back to or facing?"

"Facing, a little."

"Shit."

"What?"

"Just help me get out of here and I will explain everything I promise. I *really* can't let him see me."

"Okay okay okay. I'm going to stand up and stand in front of you. Then you're going to stand and walk beside me. Keep your face to the window and he probably won't see you."

"Okay. So, count to three?"

"Okay."

"One."

"Two."

"Three."

--

When I was maybe twelve, Janel Picket and I used to run just like how I ran from the café that night in Gyumri. We'd walk the trail down to the river, under the viaduct bridge, and psych ourselves into thinking that if we saw anyone there they'd be a molester or a serial killer. At the bottom of that rocky, steep path, under a dank bridge, only horrible people wanting to prey on us could exist. And so as soon as we heard the crack of sticks as if underfoot, we'd dart. We'd run as fast as we could not letting ourselves realize the truth, which was that there probably wasn't a reason to run in the first place. If it even had been a person it likely wasn't a dangerous one, and I think deep down we knew this. We'd run fast but never far, stopping as soon as we reached the top of the viaduct, as though that were a safer world up there, and then we'd begin to laugh.

But the difference between running to the top of the via-duct bridge and running from the cafe in Gyumri was that when I stopped running from the café in Gyumri there was no one there to laugh with me. There was no one there to even hear it.

Melik eventually caught up, breathless and with nothing to say. He took his hat from my head and placed it back on his own. In his eyes swelled something new and I recognized it as fear, or maybe anxiety, and it occurred to me that he believed I was running from a man worth fearing, someone I'd gone to Armenia to hide from. I quit laughing and muted my expression, but I didn't do anything to tell him otherwise, recognizing the convenience in having him think that way, recognizing some truth lived in it. I knew he wouldn't press for explanation. I let it just stay as it was in the air.

"I'm sorry for this," I said. "I'm sorry to drag you into this." He pointed up the road and began walking, as though to say *from this point I will lead.*

For some time, we didn't speak, just walked. Two groggy figures making our way through the green-grey night with nothing to say. And though I was mostly glad he didn't want explanation, there was also some faint signal bleating out from some deep part of me that wanted him to give the *okay* to un-pack what had occurred. But I swallowed that bleating back and found the good in not having to explain—mostly because I wasn't sure I could, really. How *did* I feel about it?

How? I don't recall regret, or even the slightest tug to go backwards to the cafe, to Eric.

No. It was funny, really. Eric coming so close and losing me before he even saw me. Eric failing, again, to really see me even as we moved in the same room. It had been so easy to lose him. As I moved further away, with each step forward into the night, I stifled the urge to laugh again. I had won. I had main-tained my invisibility, my preservation. I told myself I would deal with the overarching issue later—the issue being that Eric was there for the dodging. I swallowed hard and walked swift.

Melik and I moved in near unison, our legs a swish of buff through the green-grey. Then after some time I found something to say, something I likely would have said if we were still sitting idle in the café. "I'm sorry I won't be able to read your story."

"Why won't you?"

"Because you write in Armenian."

He laughed and pushed me on the shoulder, said, "We'll go to Aram's studio now. It will be good for you."

--

Melik told a story as we walked. A tactic for pushing our attention away from Eric, perhaps. A story about a long deceased Gyumri philosopher named G.I Gurjieff.

After Gurjieff's favorite sister died, he decided he wanted to devote himself to understanding the place of humans in the universe. He started to read books but couldn't find sufficient answers. So he left town, deciding instead to travel the world: Constantinople, Ani, the Kurdish mountains, Serbia, the Gobi Desert, the Black Sea coast. Along the way he held many jobs: selling rugs, dyeing hedgerow birds yellow and selling them as canaries, scraping coins from the bottom of fountains, faking engineer credentials and mapping railroad lines, a stint as an addiction-curing hypnotherapist. Eventually, he decided he'd gained enough self-awareness and witnessed enough to call himself a teacher. In 1917 he returned to Gyumri and found his father had been shot by the Turks. So he decided he needed to go inward to collect himself, bringing himself back to his own existence. But when he went in, everything felt like a trap. So he left town again and decided to go back in the world. First, he tried to become a British citizen but had no luck and found himself in Paris instead. Inside a dilapidated mansion sitting on acres of land, he started a school called the Institute for the Harmonious Development of Man. His students lived with him there—middle class intellectuals, some Russian refugees, those in his family who weren't killed during the genocide. He put his students to work on the land and in the kitchen. He believed in hard labor. He believed in suffering. He believed in pain. He believed in dexterity and sensitivity. He called his belief system the Work. A training to minimize daydreaming, to expand consciousness, to weaken the patterns of poor habits, to end absent-mindedness, to increase energy. He made his students dig through the landscape of the estate grounds, making pathways for walking. As they dug, he demanded the careful placement of each root and the careful extraction of weeds. As they worked, he demanded careful thinking about the appointed place of each minute on the clock, the consistent rhythm of time. If they questioned why he demanded they do as they did, he responded: *We need to clear our paths. There is no clearing without a path, not in our universe.* He made them sit through lectures about the significance of waking up, how humans were losing the ability to think for themselves. He also taught them music and dancing and they'd dance through the night. They practiced exact positions, difficult postures, mathematical prayers. They practiced pre-gridded movements from one end of the yard to another. He demanded they feel out the connection between mind and body. And while many students left, some of them woke. Some of them made it to depths of a deeper quiet, where they acquired the attention for self-observation. In these students a change came in how the light hit their eyes. Everything got brighter. When they picked up the earth in their shovel, it felt lighter. They could throw the soil further and lift their shovels higher. When they danced they no longer ran out of breath. When they sat through lectures they stayed more focused and took in more ideas. To which their teacher said, *see, you are a different human altogether now.*

--

Constructions from Aram's head covered his studio. Squiggly compositions in blacks and whites, with small interruptions of bold reds and yellows. His container syndrome, his therapy, framed on the walls, propped on worktables, lying in grids on the concrete floor. I wondered if he made these kinds of paintings in art school, if this got him labeled as 'too emotional.' Each squiggle a separate emotion, laid down like an extracted worm. Each strand, some bit of weight from Aram's head, all there for a classroom critique.

On a woven carpet in the middle of the room, Aram poured Mulberry vodka from a plastic Pepsi bottle and Melik sat next to him smoking a cigarette. They spoke Armenian in low voices, no doubt making double sure I couldn't un-code their words. But I knew they were talking about the Eric incident. They were talking about me and what they thought was my life. Maybe even my outburst on the way to the café. And when their voices grew earnest I figured they weren't in agreement about whatever it was.

It's a special kind of heart thumping, fuzzy skin feeling, watching the eyes of others narrow with focus on you, say words you can't understand. But I pretended not to notice them, moving around the room, studying the art, working to hold the weight in my own head and under my skin as steadily as I could.

"Come for your vodka," Melik said from across the room. He rose a glass to me and I sat down between them and sipped the liquid, coughing some as it burned down my throat. It felt like college, sitting between them, waiting for my earlier buzz to return, knowing I was doing all the wrong things with my time, with my body.

Melik and Aram continued in Armenian, their voices low and lethargic. I stared straight ahead. I thought I heard Melik say the words *crawl space science* and wasn't sure but imagined that could be a term difficult to translate into another language. Were they really discussing my employment? Were they that deep in to breaking me down? I let it go. Of course they were talking about me. Aram turned to me eventually, said, "Too many faces moving in and out, no firm head count."

"He means his family," Melik interjected. "The family apartment. It's more relaxing up here."

"Home." Aram shrugged.

"Home," I repeated in a confirming, soothing voice that might have come off patronizing. Intentionally so, to serve as some nuanced signal I knew Aram's family was far from being the discussion.

After some silence Aram asked, "So, you have been tested here. But have you *successfully* been tested here? Have you come to question your reality in a way you feel is sufficient?"

I was about to say something like yes, sure, but Melik burst in in Armenian. I guessed he was saying to leave me alone, so I decided not to answer.

"What do you see when you think of home, Sara? In your mind." Aram ignored whatever his friend was saying, found another question to ask. He jabbed at his head with the tip of his index finger.

"What do I see?"

"Yes?"

Melik lit a cigarette, no longer intervening. No doubt Aram was seeking out some inadvertent way of getting me to talk about the American I was running from. But I dodged it and turned my thoughts to where I was a week before. *Home.*

The visual was difficult to translate into words, even if I'd just seen some bit of it walking in front of me. I thought to describe my apartment, my own studio, the hemmed in blocks of my city, but it was a dull scene, it hardly felt worth the words. Eventually I answered. "I guess I feel like I've dragged myself here so that I can make use of my eyes and my hands, trace the physical boundaries of something so beyond myself that home looks pretty illegible. I guess home just feels like a forced thought right now. Kind of superficial."

"Superficial?"

"Yeah." I could tell right away I was digging myself into a hole but continued anyway. "I can't really think of a visual to describe home. Not here on the spot."

Aram contorted his face in a way that said, *Bullshit. You just saw a visual from home.* I offered back a flat expression that said *I'm not full of bullshit at all.*

Melik, looked into his beer. "Leave her alone."

"No I'm okay."

"The absence of something is an architecture of its own," Aram said with a somber delivery.

"Oh I like that," I said. "And I guess you are right." I finished my vodka with a hard swallow.

"What do you like?" Aram asked.

"That statement. The way that sounds."

Aram got up and began pacing. "So what absence is trapped in your head, Sara?"

I flashed him an expression that said *I know what you're doing and I'm not going to entertain it.* I knew he wanted me to peel back some layer so he might discover something— some bold colored squiggle of my own, popping off the black surface. I looked to Melik and he still had his eyes in his vodka. I wondered which of us three he felt most embarrassed for.

Aram tried again with a different question. "Tell us some-thing that is a very important memory?"

"Very important memory," I repeated.

"Yes."

I stood up and walked to a corner, pretending to study the artwork while considering what to say next. Why should I speak at all? I was near drunk again. Things could have easily sloshed out. I walked over to Melik and held my glass out for a refill. He topped me off and I went with the first thing that came to mind that felt as far away as possible from anything that might lead back to some deeper, relevant reserve in me. My headache threatened to return.

"Well. Okay. So, there was this one time skipping a day in high school, Monica, this girlfriend of mine and I made our way to Baltimore. We used to glob our lips in Vaseline and dab a shimmering blue eye shadow over that. We wore these matching white vinyl go-go boots. Ridiculous, but when I imagine her and I doing anything together that's always how we look. Blue lips and go-go boots. So this one time we were sitting in this coffee shop we used to go to and this boy came up to us, maybe he was 19 or 20, I remember he looked sort of like Kurt Cobain but less pretty. His face was blotchier. He asked us if we'd blown a smurf to get our lips like that, but when he saw we couldn't be bothered with his heckling, we just turned away and ignored him, he suddenly became nicer. We ended up talking to him for some time and I have no idea really what we talked about but I remember he took us back to the rooftop of his apartment building. We walked up this rickety ladder off the side of his kitchen window. It was amazing to see the city from up there. The tops of buildings, the harbor in the distance and the Key Bridge. It was maybe March and the wind pierced right through us. Then he, this guy that we were so ready to impress for who can say why now, convinced Monica and I to stand on the edge of the roof with him. Right there on the side of the roof, no rail. I remember we held hands and screamed a chant, something like: *you won't be able to take us down!* That's about all I remember."

I leaned down over a series of small canvases. Each thickly painted white, small wisps of pencil over each. I picked one up and half expect a scolding for touching it, but nothing happened.

After some silence, Aram said with a new brightness in his voice, "And tell me what that moment meant to you? Come on, it's okay. Dump it out."

"Dump it out?"

"Yes."

Melik stirred on the floor, whispering something to Aram in Armenian.

"What that moment meant to me? I don't know. I mean it was stupid. I guess afterward I kept thinking about how easy it would have been to die. All for impressing a stranger, I guess. And we never saw the guy again, but in retrospect a total creep, right? So many things in the world are scary. But sometimes you face them anyway. Maybe that's the point I'm getting at."

I returned the small white canvas to its spot on the floor and looked up.

"And you know, Aram, I lost my dad too. I get it. So I'm sorry."

Aram's relaxed smirk said I'd given him what he wanted. It was a different kind of smirk than earlier, maybe the professional smile of an art therapist. He'd used tactics that made something squiggle out of me and he approved. After some silence he stood up and spread his arms to offer me a hug, which I accepted. He smelled like the room, damp and smoky. He squeezed tight, near violent, and released fast. "You are okay. And you are safe here." He said it softy, giving me a giddy rush and a tinge behind my eyes, that sting of pending tears. I pressed it all back as far as it would go.

Melik bounced up from the floor, offering his energy to the situation, the hug maybe insinuating a pivot towards more tolerable and buoyant moments. The three of us stood silent for several seconds in a circle and I hoped to hear Melik say it was time to go.

Aram lost some of his smile and blinked at me. "The bliss of nobody," he said beneath his breath, as though passing on a secret. He clapped his hands together with one hard smack. "Okay let's do it. Let's go on the roof and yell something."

--

The climb to the roof from the window was easy. No rickety latter, just a small twist of the body from a wide and safely fenced ledge to the roof itself. We aligned ourselves in a row. The tang of wood burning filled the air and the cool blue hue of night inked away any sign of what existed in front of us: the mountains, the fields, Eric, the broken buildings and thousands of shitty *domiks*. Maybe it was just too peaceful up there to yell anything, I don't know, but we didn't yell anything at all. We didn't even speak. We just sat, three distinct vessels for our own special kinds of grief, perched over a world of scary things.

I waited for someone to speak the just-right words that would make this an important memory, the kind of thing we might repeat again years later, drunk with new friends. I thought to make it happen myself, to be the one to complete the composition, but the words came close and then slipped off elsewhere. I told myself it was okay. We had nothing to say to each other, but we'd climbed the same path to the same roof and now we could trace the same star lines in the sky. Again came the sting of pending tears and I pressed and I pressed.

So seldom had I known that sort of perfection. Relinquishing to the quiet.

Melik and I kept up the silence during the taxi ride back, then offered each other tired salutes good night— him a tipping of his hat and me an *aye-aye-sir*. I went straight to the courtyard, not wanting the confines of a house's rooms just yet. I'd wanted to extend the night some, keep the dark over me. I sunk into the bench, with a backdrop of night insects and the thin notes of a piano from some open window. It wasn't long before Levon came down. I said hi and he grunted his grunt, turned on the sprinkler, pulled the folded rugs from the table. He nodded his head, a motion for me to stand so he could lay a rug on the bench, a drill I knew well.

I wanted to know what might happen if I said nothing at all. If I ignored him. I wanted to know what might happen if I said I wanted to sit alone. Or, if I said that no, I wouldn't stand up, and the bench was fine as it was. But instead I sprung up, chirping out something canned, bright and cheery, some recycled utterance of compliance, something he'd come to anticipate. I told myself we were just too far in to settle into anything else. The calm of Aram's roof, the confidence to just remain quiet, didn't transfer to Levon's courtyard. And to say no, to not comply, would just cause disruption, would knock us off the expected course and into some place where Levon might be offended. In that moment I didn't have the energy to be who I'd preferred to have been, and I hated myself for that.

Under the light of a single bulb, on opposite benches, Levon and I looked past each other. He lit a cigarette, opened a bag of sunflower seeds, spreading them onto a porcelain plate. For some minutes there was just the cracking of seeds between teeth, shells spit to the ground, the insects and far off piano. He stood and signaled to the light switch. "I turn off, yes?" He turned the light off without waiting for my response.

"Okay," I said.

It was darker than I would have thought, a different kind of dark in the yard. Different than the house with the lights out or the roads at night. It was that complete black that balls up the eyes. I got knocked uneasy.

"You had a good day at work?" I squeaked out.

"Yes. Work."

"Good."

I worked to distinguish what it meant for Levon to turn the light out. What could he replace the light with? I told myself he just wanted to save money. He had found me with the light on at an unexpected hour and needed to do something to curb the expense. Or, maybe he was testing the limits of my yeses.

"My son go to London. School," he said, still cracking sunflower seeds.

"Oh. That's great. Good! When?" I kept ease in my voice, working to act as if nothing had changed.

"Maybe 30 September. He go get visa. Maybe. Maybe you help."

"How?"

"You know people."

"People? Like who?"

"You know people help with scholarship."

"Oh, I don't know about that."

My eyes adjusted to make out the lines of Levon's giant shape. The white hem of his t-shirt began separating from the blackness and I found relief in things taking shape. I'd gotten through the darkest part.

Levon rose to his feet. "Okay I sit by you."

"Sure?" My compliance tilted up in an unhinged question.

He sat next to me, lit another cigarette and dragged the ashtray toward him. We stared into the dark, silent, and I kept my limbs stiff, careful to give off no signs of comfort or invitation, not wanting to provoke, not wanting to suggest I thought he meant harm.

I knew he couldn't mean harm. I knew everything could only be fine. But then he leaned in and grasped for my arm and I leaped out of myself. I leaped out, silent, and hovered above and told myself I knew he couldn't mean harm. He rubbed his old fat booze stinking lips over my cheek and I told myself he couldn't mean harm. I felt a cool putty on me. A tiny pressing. I hovered and he found my breast. I came back. I stood.

"You can't go there, Levon. You can't do that."

My voice was slow and measured but the anger lining it could not have been mistaken.

"You can't."

I let it go again with more anger.

He sat with his head in his hands.

Play it cool now, I thought. I moved to the opposite bench, picked up a sunflower seed.

He lifted his head. "Why alone?" he asked. "You should not be alone."

And I did the only thing I could think to do from there. I lied. "Well I'll be married next year. He's coming to Armenia actually. You may meet him if you'd like to. I should have told you, but I didn't know he was coming. Decided to join me at the last minute."

"It's lonely," he said, staring out at the yard.

I doubted he'd gotten my response, and I was mostly hoping he hadn't, regretting saying it as it came out, so I let it drop rather than put in the work to have it make sense. I let us both fall quiet. We'd reached the end of our exchange. He had guided us to a dead end. The dead end of where I'd said yes too many times and he'd stretched out to find the boundary of that.

As we sat there, it sunk in that Levon hadn't questioned the *no* my body eventually made. He hadn't pushed back. Or, maybe he just didn't have the strength to follow through.

He stabbed out his cigarette on the side of the table. I could make out the trees and grass of the yard now. My eyes had found all the light there was to find.

I let just enough silence pass to a point where a transition would feel natural. Just enough silence to say that what had occurred was not the end of the world, not something to unpack. Then I rose from the seat. "Okay. I'm going to bed," I said.

And though I wanted to sprint up the stairs, I knew no good could come from it. So, I moved slow and casual, turning back to say one last thing, anything that might come to me, to firm up the transition I'd initiated. "Why don't you sleep more?"

"Because. Too dangerous."

"I'm sorry."

I found my way up the stairs in the dark.

--

You could argue: I stayed agreeable because I wanted it to begin and end gracefully.

You could argue: It was my fault. I'd decided to be there. I'd managed to steer the course.

You could argue: We are all just wounded beasts feeling our way in the dark, hoping to find each other.

--

From the bed in the spare room of Levon's house I stared at the spot where the gun and rock once sat. The blank space, the cavity I'd carved out with my presence.

Levon creaked by, and his cigarette smoke seeped under the door. He passed and shut the door to his bedroom. All was in order, the house constricting in silence, as silent as ever.

--

The night Levon grabbed me, the night I lied and said I was engaged, the night Eric almost found me, also became the night of the earthquake. A bit of one at least, far below where I lay. A small energy burst, the force of cracking rock, an unknown distance below, nudging me from shallow sleep. I oriented myself to Levon's smoke, the mumbling TV and the only other signals to say I wasn't dreaming—the wobble of water in the glass on the bedside table and the ceiling's clanking light fixture.

And then the fear, of course. That buzzing heat in the chest. I waited for his knock on my door, gripping the bed, raising the sheets, thinking to shell myself in. The light fixture settled into place. Another earthquake could follow, I thought. Can they go from tremors to larger quakes or is it only the other way around?

After some minutes I walked slowly to the window, spread the curtains. I unlatched the windows and opened them wide, scanning for signs of disaster. As far as I could tell, everything remained in disparate, quiet parts.

I'd anticipated some stirring. The faults rocking people together, neighbors going out to reach each other. But the only disruption came from within me and I began questioning if it was anything at all.

But my body had rumbled awake. I needed to get out of the room.

I leaned back toward the door and listened for signs of his stirring. The TV murmured on, so I peered out the window to gauge my distance from the ground. I guided my body down, momentarily cupping the edge.

It's the seconds before the fall that count. The last dangle at the edge.

The fall itself was an easy drop of no real distance. No shock I couldn't absorb.

With a small jump I stood under the stars. Levon had forgotten to turn the sprinkler off. I left it on, wanting to keep everything as I found it. For a few long moments I remained still, anticipating signs of him. None came. I retreated from the perimeter, picking up my easel, still leaning against the wall outside.

I passed Melik's house, the blue glow of electronics flicking through the window's white lace curtains. I slowed but didn't think to knock, didn't think to break the facade of order. I walked, head to the ground. I walked the straight shot up Tigran Mets, toward the Ghost Town. On the horizon, the moon was on its way out. I had no idea what time it was.

--

Time grants us lines to stay inside. Grids. The first clock was the sun and the moon. We just needed more.

I walked and told myself I did not need more than just that.

--

In the steppe field, I lay down my easel and supplies and sat to wait for the sun. I tried to map the dead buildings in my mind, making logic of my surroundings. A fine lip of pink began to collect ahead, the warmth of west to the left. Then out of the small soundless breeze, a howl erupted and subsided. A fine, weak and far away sound. I told myself not to fear. I told myself it was a beautiful, dark place to be, that temporary perfection, where nobody is looking for you.

If an atrocity had occurred, it would have been a small one. *Artist found mulled to death in a field by the wild dogs of Armenia. Tourist abducted while wandering in Armenia. Woman reached out too far, and got caught.*

No.

I patted my legs to see if I'd brought the house key and realized I was wearing my pocketless pajama pants. I laughed. I'd left the window open and if I started walking back I could get there before the sun came up. Levon wouldn't have to know. But I decided to stay and wait for the light.

I lay back and thought about a story Narine told me about a family living in a *domik*. The brother, the sister, the brother's wife and three small children in a two-room *domik*. After 26 years the family came up on the list for a two-bedroom flat. So the sister, who lost a leg during the earthquake, decided to stay behind. That's how you do it with two bedrooms and six family members. No government official was going to account for the changes time might make.

I told myself that when I got home I'd figure out a way to paint them with vermilion, ochre and ultra-marine. I'd take my time with oil paints, not acrylics. I'd plot out a house for them, even if I had to pluck it from my head.

What else to do with a story like that? Keep it as long as it will stay. The story will likely fade but the remnants might keep circulating through my blood.

I hoped it would.

--

When they discharged me from the hospital, my sister drove me home.

I strained to hook the seatbelt around me and my sister made a show of getting out of the car, coming around and leaning in to hook it for me.

"There we go," she said, sounding like she had just clasped a child safely into her car.

"So, what did it look like, anyway?" She asked as she started the engine.

"What did what look like?"

"The tumor!"

I said I didn't want to talk about it. Not because I didn't as much as I wanted her to know she couldn't have everything she wanted from me.

--

The little man, the tumor, consisted of approximately 7 hair follicles. That's what I counted when they placed it in my palm. It looked like a long-finished scouring pad.

I've heard that hair is just old cells tightly packed together. There are many other interesting details about hair. As with anything that makes everything—most of the details feel impossible to imagine, until they present themselves neatly in your grasp.

--

The pink lifted itself, shaping another day, the buildings began showing themselves. I waited for the howl of the dog to come back but heard nothing. The stars faded and I could see rose hips and weeds and the rocks in the dirt all around me. I collected some rocks into a pile. A pile of small rocks. I saw the impression my easel had left in the grass over the days. I saw my small record.

# 8

I knew I couldn't stay in Gyumri. Between Eric and the booze-stinking lips of Levon on my cheek, too many boundaries had been crossed, boundaries that hijacked the composition I'd set out to develop. And so walking in my pajamas with my easel under my arms, under the mounting heat of Gyumri's sun, I plotted an early dismissal.

I knocked on Melik's door. And his widening eyes, his stutter, reminded me of what I must have looked like.

"Yeah I know. It's a long story. I don't know where to begin. Did you feel that earthquake last night?"

"What's wrong? Is it the guy—"

"Everything is fine but I've kind of locked myself out of Levon's and by now he's at work and—."

"You what?"

"If you don't have a key then I'll need you to give me a lift through the window."

--

The first Armenian I became familiar with was the famous painter Arshile Gorky. Long before Narine, long before Levon and Melik, I discovered him in a high school art class. He had fled the genocide with his family, his mother had starved to death in Yerevan, he eventually ended up in America with a father he never got along with. He lived a life with ill health, injury, a cheating wife, a fire that destroyed his studio. He hung himself in his mid-forties.

I took to him, reading that his signature move was to embrace his awkwardness, something evident in his well-known self-portrait, a painting widely considered incomplete. It's a painting that reflects an exhausted, slouching figure. His eyes the shape of leaves, his arms disconnected, abstract forms, limbs trapped in a mass of paint. Some argue that the painting was purposely left unfinished, because he didn't want the challenge of drawing the hand. But some argue, and this is my preferred argument, that he purposely left his self-portrait with inarticulate forms as an illustration of how much he disfavored the distracting everyday details that orbit us so dominantly.

The distracting every day details, life's chatter, mounting pressures, those distractions not easily swatted away. These things lead me to Gorky's self-portrait.

If I'd been moved by anything in Narine's photograph, wasn't it the satisfaction in its disarray?

This was how my composition was left unfinished:

I gathered my things in a hurry. I left the payment for my stay on Levon's kitchen table and let Melik walk me to the bus depot.

I let him take care of what seemed to be the impossible task of purchasing a ticket for a van headed to Yerevan.

I dropped my luggage in the dust, hanging back from the van for as long as I could without missing the ride.

Melik picked up my things and wiped them with his t-shirt.

"Always looking out for me." I said it too slow, maybe mean. But he'd proven good at overlooking my weaker moments.

"Tell me why you climbed out the window."

"You don't want to know."

"I do."

"Didn't you feel that earthquake last night?"

"Maybe I should go with you to Yerevan. Where will you stay?"

"That's nuts. I'll stay at Emma's I think?"

"Who?"

"Or the hostel."

"Yes, Theatre Hostel, you had said. It's good there. Good people."

He had concerned eyes. The sort of eyes that left me uneasy. The kind of eyes that said my foolishness filled him with sadness.

Then I realized that Melik and I weren't going to ever see each other again. And maybe that's all his eyes were saying. Maybe it mattered, those sad eyes. Maybe the sad made sense.

"Just take care of yourself." He took out my sketchbook and wrote down his phone number. "Call me when you are in Yerevan."

I reached into my bag and handed him the painting. "I think this is meant to stay here with you."

"I understand. You can find some more interesting things for your last days here in other places. Like you say, it's all the boring light after 1p.m. now here. Yes?"

"No. But take the painting."

He concentrated his sad eyes on the canvas, held it at arm's length.

It surprised me as I did it, the relinquishing of my work. But I couldn't imagine the weight of it as I travelled. If I wasn't to complete it, I needed to leave it with someone who might keep the rest of its story in their own head. Even if I might regret parting with the painting, when I was in the mood for that sort of regret, it would be worth it if it meant Melik might remember me in a decent light.

I said, "It's funny. I thought somehow I'd look different here."

He flicked his sad eyes up to me and nodded. "Sure. Makes sense."


## *Yerevan*

On the van ride back, images of Eric festered in me. The sight of him in an Armenian café. And Levon. I felt the turn of my stomach.

How dare either of them?

It had felt like moving backwards, to leave Gyumri three days premature.

Painting had been a firm utility. A reason for being. A clean excuse I would deliver upon returning home to explain my sudden absence. But with that gone, what was there to validate my presence in that faraway country?

The steppe so reminiscent of New Mexico, the sudden appearance of Mt Ararat, the cows getting switched on the ass by the hunched women—these were things I'd likely never pass again. And really, that should have been its own firm utility.

Leaning against the van's glass, I wanted to be outside. I wanted a slow walk along the road through the steppe, letting the blisters cluster up if they came, just to get back on my own.

--

I'd dozed off and came to when the van jerked to a halt outside Yerevan's Marriot Hotel, in what I recognized to be Yerevan's Republic Square. The driver jumped out, threw the side door open and shouted in Armenian as he moved to the back to retrieve my luggage. I imagine he said something, like, *get out and fast. I'm doing you a favor by not forcing you to go all the way to the bus depot with the rest of us. You may have a hard time finding your way back here and clearly here at a fancy hotel is where you'd prefer to be.* I had kept my mouth shut through the drive but my foreignness was unavoidable.

The cool, sterile, floral smelling air of the Marriott hit like a strange paradise. It wasn't a luxury meant for me, but I let the concierge swing the glass doors wide and I took his smile and returned it as though surrounding myself with polished marble and gold and burgundy and chandeliers made sense.

I could not deny the refuge I might find from walking to the reception and ordering a luxurious room. To be alone in a clean room with Wi-Fi and water I could control the temperature of. But I followed the signs down the marble hallways for the luxurious restroom, washed my face, changed my shirt, smoothed my hair and straightened the bags on my shoulder. I worked a confidence across my face that said I belonged there and found my way to the outdoor café.

I did look like I belonged there, it was true. At least on the surface. The confirmation coming with the steady rotation of hyper-attentive, demure, crisp-shirted wait staff who took turns approaching my table, each with some command of the English language, each with their own task. There was water to fill in the glass and salt and pepper shakers to place down. And, also, the patrons around me. I couldn't say where most of them were from but clearly this was where the foreigners flocked for breakfast.

I ordered from an English menu and embraced the novelty of the Roman alphabet, but went with the cheapest / closest to an Armenian-seeming item on the menu—a lentil soup with dried apricots and walnuts.

I tapped into the swift moving Wi-Fi and considered whether or not I should contact Emma. Would that just make for an unbearable few days, to be hooked into her world? Or

would her hyper-activity and her manipulative way of swaying
me to places against my better judgement be just the right
distraction? I decided against it.

I logged into my email.

From Frannie. Subject: hey

Eric called. He thinks you're in trouble. Could you give
me a phone number for there so we can talk? Did you down-
load skype? There's some things you should know and I'd rather
express it over the phone. This ridiculous trip—

I clicked off.

From Eric. Subject: We need to meet up.

You owe me an explanation—

I clicked off.

I felt a heat run through my head. A mixing of no sleep
and the feral-animal sensation that comes when you want to
hide. I assessed the sensations running through me. I felt only
a little sharpness in my arms from hauling my luggage and the
fuzz of sleeplessness in my head.

The signs of my surgery had subsided, but maybe my fatigue was reason enough to justify hiding away for three days
in Yerevan's most expensive hotel. My bill for the soup, bread
and coffee came to about twenty US dollars and so, no. I'd
manage at the hostel.

--

Hostel Boy was there on his computer and stirred to his feet
when I walked in, laughed a small and anxious laugh, similar
to how he had the day I arrived.

"Yes, okay. You are here again. And you are lucky we have
your room again. How was the painting for you in Gyumri?"

"I left the painting there, for better or for worse, we'll see.
But yeah it was really good. Really great place."

His flat expression signaled that I exhibited the wrong amount of enthusiasm over Gyumri, or I had failed to exhibit the correct amount of gratitude that my room was available, or maybe I'd used words he struggled to understand. Most likely he just knew how silly it sounded to call Gyumri *a really great place.*

"I'm afraid I'm quite tired right now. I was up all night. You know there was a tremor last night I think?"

His face finally broke. "Oh, Melik!"

"Melik?"

"Of course." He took his phone off the desk and began scrolling through. "He said you may come and so when you are here he wants to know. He just called, really. Wants to speak. No problem."

"How do you know Melik?"

"These are small towns you travel."

I felt a brightness to know that he was looking out for me even after I'd vanished. Unlike Eric, I trusted he knew where to draw the line, how far to follow me and from what distance.

Melik answered on one ring, said "I need to let you know what just happened this morning."

--

What happened after I'd left was that Melik had walked over to Aram's.

It was Aram, Melik said, who was responsible for things going wrong when they crossed paths with Eric in the square, for telling Eric that he should stay away from me, leave me alone, leave the country, quite abusing women altogether, be a better American.

Eric had his own explanations and defenses, came back saying they had no idea who I really was. Whatever I'd said about him I'd lied, held back, pretended I was better off than I was. I was fragile and no doubt I'd concealed it from them, having just had surgery, having left without a doctor's clearance. I had a history of making poor decisions.

I paused to consider what he meant by *poor decisions*. If it was an exact quote.

"And what did you say back?" I asked Melik, my heart beginning to bang in my throat.

"Well. So, we told him we would arrange for you to see him. That I would know how to reach you and arrange a meeting. Don't worry it was just something we told him. Like a joke.

"Hilarious, Melik."

"We didn't know what to say. He was begging us. Sorry. He did seem very serious though. I mean, like, he cared. He did come all the way here for you so maybe you should think about contacting him. Let him know yourself that you are safe."

I laughed hard into the phone. I could almost see the chance meeting. Aram's intensity and Eric's hostile defensiveness transitioning into smooth charm and manipulation.

"What time did you tell him I would meet him?"

"3 at the Russian restaurant."

"Well I think I'll let him have a few hours of looking forward to seeing me then."

For a minute, just silence on the line. Something would unfold that I could stop—Melik's silence said as much. I knew he knew that if I wanted, if I made an immediate decision to do so, I could likely get back to Gyumri by 3. My heart banged harder.

"Melik, Eric set himself up for this one. He'll need to take what's coming. Not my responsibility. Sorry to get you caught up in this, though."

"It's okay. But also you should know that Levon is upset, too. Mostly about the gun and the rock he says."

"That I understand."

After hanging up I caught Hostel Boy's face twitching at me, his thin smile. Melik had given him the backstory.

"Everything is fine," I sighed out.

He lowered himself back into his chair and returned to his computer screen.

"Suggestions on what I should do in Yerevan?"

"Tours," he said without missing beat, leaning to a box of brochures on the counter. "There are some tours at the tour agency at the next building. Buses go every day to new towns."

--

I'd eventually hear from my mother that the military was not my father's first choice after all. It had been art. But his family dissuaded him.

She'd told me this drunk at a holiday dinner.

"Unlike you there was nobody there to pay for his art school. Think about that," she said. "Think about that next time you are feeling sorry for yourself."

I always assumed my father would have been disappointed if I hadn't pursued art. Or, if I had abandoned art, I think he would have wanted me to do something spectacular, as he had. Break the sound barrier for a living, soar high.

# 9

I woke with the first crack of light in my room in the hostel and thought about how barriers come in all shapes and sizes, as does the manner in which they get broken.

--

There was a bus tour heading to Nagorno-Karabakh, departing at 7 a.m.. I signed up. We'd be staying overnight at Hotel Europe in the capital city of Stepanakert, making several stops along the way at what the bright faced young woman at the tour desk described as *very important Armenian historical sights*.

It was the poster covering the tour's office door that convinced me. The monument of the man and woman chiseled out of pink volcanic stone, half-buried in the earth, the sunny blue sky, the crisp green grass, the monument where Levon's family had posed on vacation. Some happy fortress on a sunny hill—a benign sunniness that conflicted with the sun I'd experienced for the previous week.

I knew very little about Nagorno-Karabakh, but I'd skimmed *Lonely Planet* after Narine had mentioned it vaguely in conversation. I knew it was a kidney shaped bit of land on the Azerbaijan border. That's how it was described. A kidney. A vulnerable organ.

To say *vulnerable* is no stretch: it is a disputed territory, once conquered by Arab Muslims, once conquered by Imperial Russia, then—and still—fought over by Azerbaijan and Armenia. A dense ball of conflict between empires and states and regions, nestled high in the mountains. De facto independent. As *Lonely Planet* had said: *a self-declared republic recognized by no one.*

The Azerbaijan border. The border Eric stressed to stay far from in his email. That made it all the more appealing. To report back that'd I'd faced an imminent danger would be worth it. And it made sense to wind up mountain roads and end up somewhere de facto independent. Where I'd gone so far to search for it hadn't proved far enough.

I boarded the tour bus and an ease ran through my shoulders as I slinked into the air conditioning and plushy blue seat. The bus was far from full and with just minutes before departure time I hoped that it would remain so. I leaned my knees against the back of the empty seat in front of me, curled in on myself, waited to rumble off into the mountains.

There was that last minute shuffling. Luggage was too large to fit in the overhead compartment and would need to go under the bus, someone forgot to have their passport copied for the office files. In what I assumed was the routine scene of a tour group preparing to disembark, a scene occurring all across the world, the second thoughts sunk in. I scanned my fellow travelers. Everyone clumped in pairs or groups. With sun hats and proper foot-wear, water bottles and bags of snacks. They'd likely done this before.

What was the good in it for me?

To occupy my time, to not be in Yerevan, to get away from Eric, to not answer Frannie's email. I'd chosen this.

Lucine would be our guide. She came on board with a stomp up the stairs, her thick red curls tucked loosely under a large straw sun hat garnished with fiery red plastic flowers. She had a muscular voice, as she read our names from a clipboard, speaking first in English, then Russian, letting us know of all agenda details, letting us know that cakes and waters would be available at all times. Everything about her said she would take charge but would do so while ensuring we had a fun and safe time and above all, she would be difficult to miss in a crowd. She pointed to her head. "Just look for this," she said. We'd be buoyed by her large hat and large voice.

Lucine took the front seat, she spoke through a microphone, which felt wrong at that early hour, for a voice so strong on its own.

"We first stop at Gerghard Monastery. And we are off with many great things to see and learn!"

Rolling through Yerevan, I could almost trace the route, passing familiar bakeries and fruit stands, passing familiar scenes of old men crowded around wooden chess boards, watermelon piles, it seemed like a city with one point of entry and exit.

On the outskirts, back into the moonscape, Lucine raised and steadied in the front of the aisle, continued with the microphone, first in English, then Russian.

"You should know about New Aleppo; do you know about New Aleppo?" She fixed on the middle aged, khaki-clad couple seated directly behind her. They mumbled back. I'd done right to choose the back half of the bus.

"So I will tell you. Soon there will be apartments here." She pointed to some dry earth. Some sheep grazed the brown.

"They had to leave a century ago because of Turkey. No doubt you of course know about Turkey and the genocide but I will tell you that there was a time when Armenians made their way to Syria, which as you know is no place to be now and so now these families are making their way back here and they are getting Armenian passports once again. Some have come back to their ancient homeland with nothing but what they wear the day they leave. It is better for them here than tent cities along the sea, as you can know. And now they come here with great skills and exotic spices. First they had gone to Syria and now they come back to Armenia. One place is always better than the other. Soon they will build apartments here."

*One place is always better than the other.* I wondered if this was an Armenian proverb. I pictured the world's map. We were so close to Syria, something I hadn't thought much about.

I wondered if anyone back home really knew exactly where I was on the map. Probably not. I thought of Eric. We'd never gone further than New York together, never even talked about it. In our short time, going away had rarely seemed realistic—not on my salary, not with his work.

Was he working in Armenia? Of course he was. But how? And how well?

I could count the number of times Eric asked me about my own job on one hand. For much of our relationship I had not been phased by this, finding my job a dull topic anyway.

It generally came out as a small question that quickly drifted away. His formula: start a monologue of details about his laborious day, chiseled out deals, challenges, conversations. Pause for my appropriate serving of concern. And if left-over energy presented itself to Eric after his performance of despair, he'd ask about my own job. And since my job was as small and unimportant as his question, listening to the response never required much effort.

But one time, toward the end, one morning over coffee, he asked "What's going on with you at work?" with the stilted concern of a therapist.

I rolled my eyes. "Not much to report, really."

He lowered his cup and reached for my hand, "If you've got so much disdain for it, why don't you do something else?

I believe that deep down you've got the self-esteem to do it. Really."

I let my hand slowly retreat into my lap.

"Deep down? What makes you think I'm there because I lack self-esteem?"

"Of course not." He slurped his coffee and flashed the smile of a horrible and attractive person who thinks of himself as a gift to the world.

"Deep down?"

"Think about it."

"No you—"

"No, really think about it and then, you know, we can come back to the topic." He winked at me from behind his coffee cup, found my leg under the table, rubbed it softly with his.

I watched myself dissipate in the moment, buttoned into his opinions. There was no room for me to talk, breath, be.

I hoped that hunting for me in Armenia was disrupting his work. I hoped he was losing himself to the chase, scattered and absent from his life.

I turned to the window, focused on the steppe. Leaned my cheek to the cool glass. How shallow to stray from thoughts of Syria to Eric.

I focused on Lucine as she explained how a mountain on the horizon was shaped just like a sleeping person. She switched over to Russian before I could make much sense of it. I couldn't see anyone.

--

Narine had said it was a fact that I wouldn't be able to avoid going to at least one monastery, if not more than I would care to see. She'd said this with a warmth in her eyes even while spitting out the words in a way that signaled she did not find pride in the fact. It hadn't really registered, just what she meant by monastery.

According to Lucine, Gerghard Monastery was carved into the side of a mountain by Gregory the Illuminator in the 4th Century. The name translates into Monastery of the Spear, referring to the spear that wounded Jesus at the Crucifixion. The spear being a relic reportedly housed at the monastery for centuries, making it a pilgrimage site. I wanted to ask what happened to the spear, but didn't want to break my silence.

Climbing the switch back toward the Monastery, Lucine said, "Now it will be important when we stop that you only go so far as you can because it will be very hot and you will need water and please be careful. And please feel free to buy some dried fruits and some breads from the women who will sell them at the entrance. We have thirty minutes."

On our descent to the bus, Lucine handed me a cake and bottle of water. Up close she looked younger than I'd initially thought. Her makeup glistening in the heat and threatened to run down her wide cheeks.

"Are you okay?" she asked me with a smile.

I blew out an uncomfortable laugh. "Yes. Of course."

Maybe I had studied her too long, or maybe I looked unwell. What else did she see in my face?

I took my sketchbook to a stone wall with a view of what I thought was the sleeping person mountain.

"Behind you again." Came a voice, laughing.

I could smell them before turning around. The two men who'd sat at the back of the bus. Too much cologne for such a small space. One unusually tall, the other unusually short—height being the best marker to distinguish them, given their otherwise nearly mirrored appearance. Crisp designer-looking jeans, leather shoes, Ray-Bans. I sensed that they too were not the guided tour type.

"We were behind you on the bus," the taller one said, dissecting the joke.

"God I wish I could do that. Shit," said the shorter one, pointing to my sketchbook.

"Thanks." I made some attempt to work a buoyancy into the word before turning back around.

I learned long ago that to make art in public was to offer yourself up for critique, to invite a lack of control in how the experience took shape.

I longed for Ghost Town and Melik.

"Fruit?" The taller one stuck out a bag of dried apricots.

The gesture marked the point of a decision. To engage or not. I reached out my hand for some fruit, gritting my teeth.

The shorter one lifted his sunglasses to look at the drawing. "Let me see that?"

I held up the drawing, which wasn't much more than some brisk lines at that point. He glanced down at it and then looked up at me, blank-faced. His dark almond eyes could have been Armenian.

"*That's* really fucking amazing. I mean we've been here for like ten minutes."

"You could probably, like, move here and sell these at the gate," said the tall one.

"I might."

They both laughed too hard.

"Are you a volunteer?" Asked the short one.

"Volunteer?"

"Yeah, you know a lot of young American women come here because they volunteer."

"It's about the only reason," chimed in the tall one.

"No. You?"

"Hell no, no attorneys." They said *attorneys* in near unison. They said it casual as though of course they were attorneys.

"Real estate," said the tall one.

"You do real estate?"

"No legal real estate. Foreclosure defense."

"Attorneys for real estate?"

"Yes. Now you got it," said the short one.

"Nice," I lied, trying to use the simple, flattering word as a punctuation. Some chance to turn away. But they were not letting me go.

"So you're here to be an artist," said the short one.

I dropped my pencil, turned around, placed the book on the wall.

"Weird?"

"Yeah."

"Well, I've been working on a big project in Gyumri and I just decided to switch up the scenery a bit."

"Gyumri?"

The tall one began to drift toward someone selling trinkets some feet away.

"I'm from Gyumri," said the short one, a new sober tone.

"Really?"

"You were in Gyumri? Why the hell?"

"I have a friend from there."

"I left after the earthquake."

"Oh wow. I—"

"Yeah, you know ten days after. Man, you came here to go to *Gyumri* to make *art*? And by yourself? Not with, like, a program or something?"

"Yep. Sorry about the earthquake, I mean— "

"Yeah, yeah." He shook his hand at me and put his sunglasses back on. "It's all good."

His tall friend watched him walk away. "Yeah he won't go back. Came all the way here after all that time and won't go back."

"Sorry."

"Sorry? Why sorry? Hell, you're an artist. I mean, that's an interesting place to work I guess right?"

"I guess."

"You *guess?*"

"Sure."

He snickered under his breath and walked away.

--

Narine said, to some, God disappeared after the earthquake. Like a star sucked up in a black hole. The absence felt like stumbling into the knowledge of what nothing is. Or, some said, no he is here. Here and as indifferent as the rock that fell on our heads. Hard and heavy and just as dumb. Some said, God is still here, the great betrayer, still hanging over us, even if he no longer touches us. A perpetual, invisible action arching above. Low but far out of reach. Some said, no it's just another day with God. Like any other day, like tomorrow. Some protected God. Some said: *don't blame him, it's nature's fault. God would never be so cruel. Only nature could bring such destruction.* Some were not occupied with God or even nature at all. Their minds were jammed with memories of better days and questions of what could have been, what should have been. Some orbited between all these theories about God, never landing on any of them. God was and he wasn't. They blamed him and they didn't.

Narine believed it was easier thousands of years ago, when the sun was God. There was a time people sacrificed horses to keep the sun happy. At least you could see what you worshipped, even if looking would make you blind.

Narine told me, "You are going to go see it all for yourself."

--

Sorry.

*Why sorry.*

I looked out over the wall at the mountains and was re-minded of an essay from college. Linda Nochlin's 1971 essay, "Why Have There Been No Great Women Artists?." At it's core, it advocates for women to take risks. To create some-thing the world is going to care about, an artist must be sin-gle-minded and selfish, be able to shrug off self-pity and break from the confines. Not be so eager to apologize for herself.

I looked out over the wall at the mountains and felt my face heating. It was the heat of anger, and sadness, and embar-rassment. The slow burn of guilt.

How was I to break through any confine, shrug off any pity, embrace any self-absorption when I found it so easy to say *sorry*. Why was I so ready to claim ownership for the emotions of another, or to assume the blame?

And by jumping on the guided tour I'd built myself a perfect cage, the ultimate constriction. By nature, the bus tour is a framed experience. My name on a clip board. My passport photocopied. Cakes and water available at all times. A bus that might not move without me. I let myself cry for just one minute.

--

We took increasingly steep switchbacks, my ears crackling as we gained elevation, my legs tingling from sitting. The terrain got stonier, the rocks got larger. In my head that harsh land-scape illustrated the forbidden. My thoughts swung to Narine and I thought about what I would say about my detour away from Gyumri. Would I offend her? I slumped in my seat, tried to shake off my anxiety, the leftover ugly heat generated by my interaction with the real estate lawyers.

We were heading toward the Azerbaijan border. And nestled in my seat, on a large air conditioned bus, rolling passed the jagged landscape, I wanted nothing more than to move deeper into it—past the clear and established limits, to break new ones.

I felt the slightest spike of pain in my side. A faint shock that ran from my gut down to my knee. But the sensation lacked confidence. I rubbed the inside of my leg. *Take control,* I told myself.

--

I'd been on such a tour bus only one other time, with my family in Tulum, Mexico, when we'd left our week long all-inclusive compound to tour the Maya ruins for a day.

With me about to graduate college and Frannie just beginning, we would both be out of the house for good. I think it was Charlie's idea, to mark the transition with a family vacation, an out-of-character move, the only family trip we'd taken beyond state lines.

What I remember most of those seven days is the night the four of us drank too much fruity alcohol. After dinner, sitting on a slick, coral colored patio, our burnt skin sticking to blue foam lawn chairs. The white moon flickered over the Atlantic.

It was Charlie that forced the conversation to turn, as he tended to do when drinking. And I can't remember from what he turned but for some reason he referenced how our father had been adopted.

"Shut up," said our mother, weak and under her breath.

He went to these tacky places in a conversation to show that he didn't mind talking about our past. That he knew about the decisions his wife had made, all the ways he could have never come into our life as if knowing meant he could own the past. He made himself look foolish and I almost felt sorry for him. It upset our mother, I knew from her flushed cheeks and tight lips, even if she never admitted it. But it was his take on The Affectionate Drunk, and maybe that's why she let it go.

Frannie always suggested Charlie's behavior was a means of bridging the gap between him and myself, that it was really all about me. He thought he was being sensitive by bringing our father into the moment. But saw this as his way of getting at me rather than relating to me.

Frannie and I had not known our father had been adopted.

"They don't know?" he said.

"No, they didn't know," our mother said flatly.

Charlie didn't ease up, mentioned that my sister and I should consider genetic screenings.

"The girls could find out their roots."

Our mother laughed.

Frannie chimed in that it was a great idea. How fun it would be.

I silently decided those seven days in Mexico would be the end of my thin, weak roots, but I didn't need to sink deeper. I would uproot, let myself drift.

I haven't talked to Charlie or my mother in years. Making that decision was how I first learned I could cinch myself into selfishness, doing what I thought was best for me and not others.

--

We descended and things got green again. The road broadened and smoothed out. We passed familiar sites. Field reapers and hay triangles. Things seemed lush and wet. Lucine let us know we'd be stopping for lunch and, as though on que, a woman near the front began to sing something soft, operatic.

A floating, sweet voice, bare in the air. A strange moment that made me think this would never happen again. That sound in that spot floating back to me. For those few moments I floated as light as that sound.

That sound. That was what it was all for. The journey happened for a sound like that. Some singular voice in some singular moment for some singular lightness that could not sustain itself forever. A lightness that needed to be carried away.

--

At an outdoor fish restaurant, a maze of raw pine patios connected by bridges along an aggressive-moving river, we were placed at a large, raw pine table. We scooped chunks of mild white sturgeon, potatoes, and tomato and cucumber salad from family-style platters. The food cleared my head and I tried to remain polite while stuffing in as much as possible. It felt like it'd been days since I'd eaten.

I sat next to an Armenian American woman from Los Angeles whose name I may have never learned. She had the most perfectly manicured lavender nails and plum colored curls. She asked where I was from and when I told her D.C. she proceeded to tell me how she'd lived there in a hotel for a month, accompanying her husband on a business trip. She told me with zeal how she'd shopped every day, and each morning and afternoon the doorman asked how it was her husband let her get away with all that spending. Her husband, sitting across from us, laughed and nodded, confirming the story. I mustered a laugh to stay in the moment but I'd left myself back on the bus, in a more grounded and quiet place.

After eating, she beckoned me to the river.

"Take a film of me," she said, handing me her I Phone, fluffing up her plum hair.

"Stand there, please," she said, sweetly assertive, instructing me as a mother might. I pushed play and began to film, recording her at the edge of the river while she said something shrill in Armenian, jumping in place, boisterous, pointing at the water.

Afterward, running back to me, near breathless, "It looks good?" she asks.

"Yes, I said. Your happiness looks perfect."

--

Standing along the river, an Armenian man approached me, someone I recognized from the bus. A tall lanky man, almost dancing with every move. At lunch he'd sat at the other end of the table, the louder end, where vodka had been ordered.

"You come here to be an artist in Gyumri?" He jangled around me, vodka heavy on his breath, a deep pink lining his eyes.

I paused, wondering for a moment if I could lie.

"Yes, I am."

"Beautiful. You…"

He trailed off, unsteady on his feet.

"I'm in Tehran now," he said. "You must know of Grigorian. You must." Then he wandered down the river with his uneasy gait.

What had those real estate lawyers said? I felt my lunch turning in my stomach.

--

Grigorian. I looked him up when I could. His family fled the city of Kars in 1920, escaping the Turks and eventually ending up in Iran. He studied in Rome, opened up a gallery in Tehran. A modernist pop artist, he liked what some website described as *ordinary objects*. He experimented with earth art in Iran.

Soil compounds, mud, resin. Much of what he did looked like cracked, dry earth. Subtle ripples and eruptions on a surface. Quiet and muted, he rearranged elements of the earth for the sake of something modern. It looked like Gyumri.

I didn't find much in the way of criticism or deep explanation of his work, not in English at least, but I did find an article in the magazine *Art and Design* that referenced him. It opened by saying that as westerners we couldn't be more wrong, to think that we are the ones who are creating art while the east "waits, like a grateful beggar, for a nourishing handout." It proclaimed that "Europe and America are barely awake."

It was a statement that felt pretentious, like a pose, a writerly devise trying too hard to assert itself as an authority. But I knew better. I knew it could be true.

Brushing up against the real estate lawyers. Eating lunch with wealthy diaspora travelers. Wearing the same clothes I'd worn for a week—I began to see the haze of a wrong that can't be traveled to but that hovers around the privileged. I was seeing it clearer and clearer.

--

On the bus, dozing, I felt someone behind me, smelled the cologne.

"Hey." The real estate lawyer from Gyumri held out a plastic bottle of something. "Mulberry vodka. Go head. It doesn't bite."

I could smell the sour of it on his breath. "I should hope it won't," I said.

His friend laughed, still at the back of the bus, his feet propped on the seat, jutting into the isle.

"You sell a lot?" He said, filling up a small plastic cup with vodka.

"Art? Sure." I stretched the truth, it didn't matter.

"You selling your earthquake paintings? How much?"

I felt it come and couldn't stop it. It came from my throat fast and terrible. "I am not responsible for your pain."

"Drama," he said.

He retreated to the back of the bus before I had time to triage. I scanned for witnesses but nobody seemed tuned in. I wondered what he'd have to say about me at the next meal.

## Nagorno-Karabakh

After a couple of quiet hours we crossed the border, hitting a flatter, more barren landscape, dotted by an occasional farm. At one point the bus brakes jerked and hundreds of dingy sheep meandered across the road, sending several passengers on the bus stumbling toward the front to capture it on their phones.

Eventually Lucine announced our next stop: The Hellenistic ruins of Tigranakert, likely dating back to 120s-80s B.C., uncovered from the earth by archeologists in 2005 and currently in a suspended state of excavation, waiting additional funding.

"We will see great walls and ornamental ruins," Lucine said in a voice still as strong as it had been when we left Yerevan. I wondered how she managed to keep it going all day.

"But first, as we approach, you must look to your right to see the evidence of our more new ruins."

The ground went charred, and in the distance the remnants of buildings began to appear along a grid of vacant roads.

"Over there we see what is Agdam. You should know that Azerbaijan held Agdam but Armenian forces took it back in 1993. But there was the Nagorno-Karabakh war for it, so the citizens had to go other places. Some 28,000 peoples."

This was the disputed land between Azerbaijan and Na-gorno-Karabakh. Heavily shelled land. The dug-out trenches still well defined and rippled along the road.

"It is still used as a strategic point. And it is a ghost town so we will not go there. Oh and so you know, Tigranakert has a café."

*Ghost town.* The words washed over me as a wave. There was so much to call ghostly, so many layers of abandonment.

--

Tigranakert sat directly across the street. I waited for the bus to empty, trailing behind the others as we walked up the hill to the fortress, letting anyone who might want to speak to me have a more difficult time doing so. I passed the foundation of an ancient church and strewn ornamental stone, many labeled with a long sequence of chalky numbers. A suspended project of fitting together the past to make sense of it.

I went to the top of the fortress and looked down across the highway at Agdam. I was most attracted to it there, looking out at that vastness, the color of decay. A rusting metal green bus shelter sat along the road. Was it still functioning? An old diesel truck went by trailing a toxic black cloud. The metal green of the shelter popped out of the otherwise monochromatic landscape, as though seen through a wash. The sun was just beginning to descend. The war with Azerbaijan was even fresher than the earthquake in Gyumri, but the destruction felt older without people living among the ruins, reshaping a life with them.

This was where Eric told me not to go. This patch of earth holding so many layers of war and living.

Something electric ran through me: I'd gotten off easy. I had carried all my baggage from ghost town to ghost town. How lucky I was for the chance.

I tried to recall my boring life. The soft plodding of the hours. What it looked like day to day. But it was getting harder to see.

*Agdam*, it even sounded post-apocalyptic or like science fiction to my American ears. I'd learn later that it's an Azeri word meaning *bright sun-lit, white house*. The people who had fled had been Azerbaijanis, forced to flee by the Armenian forces.

There is never just one angle from which to compose an understanding.

--

The sun was gone by the time we approached Stepanakert. I didn't understand how the bus driver managed to stay on the steep roads. I thought we'd fall off the edge. And then ahead of us, the white blinks of city lights sprang to view.

Hotel Europe sat in the middle of a quiet town. A large sprawling hotel largely made of blue reflecting glass and white tiles, reminiscent of brutalist architecture. Lucine lined us up single file as we entered the empty, stark white lobby, fatigue creeping into her voice. We were checked in one by one without ceremony and, standing in line, I heard the real estate lawyers not far behind me. They seemed always to be just behind me, my stomach always lurching at the sound of their voices. Did they plan it that way?

"We should find the bar," one said to the other. "Lucine, where's the bar district?"

Lucine laughed brightly and said nothing.

--

My room had internet, so I logged on to find an email from Eric, only an hour old.

Subject: I am zeroing in on you.

There was no text. I laughed and turned off the IPad. He must have been drinking. Did he see Melik and Aram at 3 p.m.? I hated to think they'd hit it off. Eric was only supposed to come up against resistance with every turn in Armenia. If there was any universal justice he'd be leaving lonely, tired, desperate. He'd already be in the air headed west.

But, no.

I took a mini of vodka from the fridge and emptied it into a plastic bathroom cup.

I turned on the television to find a handful of blurry channels that sounded like they were in Russian. I squinted at the fuzzing images of Western Asian actors performing dramas I would never unlock.

I turned the IPad on again and clicked on Eric's message. Without overthinking it, I typed out a message:

Meet me at the outdoor café at the Yerevan Marriott tomorrow at 6 p.m..

It was a means of appeasement maybe. It was a means of buying time. It was a means of taking hold of the leverage. Yes, that. It was a means of talking hold of the leverage I'd gone all that way to get. I'd plot my next step later.

--

I woke with a start to a hard knocking at my door. Lucine stood there in a jogging suit, looking something between afraid and mad.

"Is everything okay?" I asked.

"It's Sara yes?"

"Yes, what's wrong?"

"I'm afraid that the police have received a call for you."

"The police?"

"Yes, downstairs. I am afraid that they have come because your husband is worried for you since you have run away here."

"My husband?"

"Yes, your husband. Please. You can take some minutes to get dressed and gather your things and then you can come down stairs to meet them."

"To meet my husband?"

"No you can meet the police men who your husband contacted. Your husband is in Yerevan."

"But I don't have a husband."

Lucine's face sagged. Accepting the idea that I had no husband didn't fit the moment for her.

"Down the stairs, please." she said.

"He's not my husband. He's—"

"Please," she begged, her voice rattled, desperate.

I decided not to resist. It wasn't her fault.

--

Two officers stood at the elevator, ready to take me down to the lobby. There was a blankness to them both. Avoiding eye contact and silent, they were the neutral bodies looking to move me from a point to a point, with a series of hand gestures, down the hall, into the elevator, through the empty lobby door and into the back of a police car. I kept silent, too. I wore nothing on my face that might reflect the banging of my heart in my throat. Lucine had retreated at some point, unnoticed—I don't think she even got in the elevator. It was 2:14 a.m. according to the clock in the police car.

How was it that Eric managed to put so many people in motion at such an hour, all for the sake of seeing me forfeit control?

I immediately regretted leaving the hotel room. Why hadn't I resisted? Why hadn't I repeated it until Lucine came over to my side? *He is not my husband he is not my husband he is not my husband.*

--

"He is not my husband."

I sobbed it at the officers as they hand-gestured me to the tan couch in the corner of a tan office. Less so a police station and more an office reminiscent of my own boring place of employment. Cream carpeted, desked, smelling faintly of old paper and dust.

"He is not my husband." I stretched the words out, slow and loud.

The officers looked at the carpet, uncomfortable with my tears, no doubt. One of them slipped out and returned quickly. He held out a delicate china cup full of coffee with a smile and when I didn't take it he placed it on an end table. Then they both left the room, shutting the door softly as though to empathize the delicate manner in which they handled me. I was worthy of their delicate china cups, their delicate door closing. I was a kit-glove containment. Or, maybe they handled everyone that way—not just sobbing American girls.

With a jut of my elbow I pushed the coffee cup from the table and for some minutes stared as the coffee seeped onto the cream carpet. The cup hadn't broken, at least. Hadn't made a sound to beckon anyone to my small outburst.

I found the door unlocked and opened it to find an empty hall ahead of me. The smell of coffee, the only evidence of any activity.

I could leave. I had a choice. So, I started toward the entrance.

Then a voice behind me. "Hey hey, no you. Sara? It's Sara, yes?"

It was a different officer, an older man.

"You speak English?"

"Yes, yes, I do, Sara. Sara, you should be back in the room enjoying your coffee. You were given coffee, yes?"

"Yes, but this isn't right. I'm afraid you have this wrong. You're wasting your time. I am not married to Eric. He is not my husband. He's just a creepy ex and he has no right." I felt my voice rise, my heart returning to my throat. I pressed under my eyes, wondered how the crying had left my face.

The officer's face held the softness that comes with concern. "Let us take you back in the room to have this conversation."

"No thank you," I said.

I continued down the hall, found the front door unlocked and made my way out. The night was so dark and quiet it felt blank. Then the door swung open, and the hall's light gave shape to the hedges skirting the building.

"Where will you go?" said the officer from behind, standing in the entrance. "Your husband has reported you because he is very concerned about your medical condition."

My blood buzzed in my head, and I filled in the blanks: Eric had talked to Hostel Boy, by way of Melik. He'd fed everyone his lie and brought them to his side. But how was it so easy for them to believe him?

"This is a mistake."

"My name is Hovhannes," he said.

"This is not right. He is just trying to find me because he is upset. He's not who he says he is. I'm doing nothing wrong."

"Yes, this is not about you doing wrong but we do want you to be safe. We understand that you have not been healthy and we want to make sure you do not hurt yourself."

"Hurt myself? No, this is wrong. This is all wrong." I felt my voice losing traction, my thighs shaking.

"Perhaps you can just lay down in the office on the couch until morning for a rest. It may not be good for you to move so much."

"What did he say was wrong with me?"

"Why did you come here, dear?"

I went with what came first. "I wanted to think of something else for a while."

Hovhannes tilted his head, as though to take me in from another angle, in some effort to make sense of me.

"May I use the phone?"

"Yes, yes, of course Sara you will want to talk to him."

I took to the couch, took another offered cup of coffee. Hovhannes pulled up a rolling chair from a desk and sat. For what felt like much longer than it probably was, we sat in silence, drinking coffee. I dodged his soft face, keeping my own to the cream carpet.

Eventually he picked up a phone from the desk, punched a couple numbers before handing me the phone.

"You will be taken to Yerevan in the morning. I promise everything will be okay. You will see your husband there and you can work it all out I am sure."

It sickened me that he thought I'd want to talk to Eric, but didn't tell him as much in case he changed his mind about me making a call.

I shifted through my bag to find Melik's number in my sketch book, but it wasn't yet light out. I would only be a disturbance. And what could he really do, anyway?

I dialed the only number I knew and Frannie answered with a quizzical sound in her voice.

"Hello?"

"I'm in a fucking Armenian jail because of you," I said over the crackling line. "You need to call him and make him stop. Tell him to go home. I've done nothing wrong and I'm not sorry about anything."

There was silence on the other line and for a moment I thought I'd lost the connection.

"You don't have to be sorry," she eventually said.

"You don't really mean that."

"The reality is that you only have yourself to blame for all your life's anger. You know that right? I didn't kill dad. Mom didn't kill dad. Charlie didn't kill dad. And you know you just had to tell us. You just needed to tell us you were going and this wouldn't be a problem. There are a lot of reasons we worry. We care. What is it that you think you're running from anyway?"

"Let me ask you this, don't you think it's kinda weird that Eric would fly all the way out here? And you're saying he came all this way because I didn't tell you two what I was doing in the first place? I mean, don't you think that's pretty extreme behavior? You do remember I broke up with him, right?

"I mean, yeah, sure, it's extreme. But maybe you could just as easily call it chivalrous or romantic. Wait. Is Eric with you?"

I did the only thing I knew how to do and hung up.

--

There was a moment at Rose's birthday party, in those twenty minutes there with Eric, which made sense only later. At least for someone as naïve as I had been.

I had hovered over the children's table and pretended to look like I belonged—no new strategy for me, especially at social affairs. But none of the adults were taking to me, seeing me as the outsider that I was, no doubt counselled by Rose's mother and rightfully so. I thought to say something to Rose but realized I wasn't quite sure which one she was of the dozen kids at the table. And I wasn't sure what there even was to say. So I let it go, standing there wringing my hands. In the kitchen

I heard the strain in Eric's voice. I heard his ex-girlfriend, the mother of his child, shrill. I don't know what they said only that there was such hurt in her voice. How could there not be? He had won. He'd made it his day.

\-\-

I lay on the couch, closed my eyes to black it all out. My body on a couch in a police office in Nagorno-Karabakh. I brought my taught knees to my chest and a heat ran through my spine, clung to my joints—the heat that comes when we pull in on ourselves, on our damage. The tears came back.

# 10

I woke to one of the hand gesturing officers, gesturing me to the next point. Another room down the hall, where Hovhannes sat at a long table having breakfast, along with the other hand-gesturer and a woman officer.

Whereas the men appeared disheveled—having shed some layers of their uniform, signaling they were coming off duty—she wore her full uniform, fresh make up, a black A line skirt, black boots and black nylons. She smiled as I entered the room and stood up to shake my hand.

"Alisa," she said, and slowly blinked her eyes. It was the blink I'd encountered a lot over those last several days, especially from women. I understood it to mean: *I am acknowledging you warmly but I do not speak your language, the conversation ends here.*

Alisa sat back down and pointed to the table, a spread of bread, cheeses and meats. It was a breakfast table reminiscent of Levon's. I thought of him—he was probably in his kitchen frying his eggs that very minute. His hair wet and his slacks on. I was surprised by a wave of sadness.

"Yes, please," said Hovhannes, pulling out an empty seat, pointing to an empty plate made from the same elegant chinaware as the coffee cups.

"Please I insist Sarah you must eat something," Hovhannes said.

I asked for a bathroom and expected an escort, but Hovhannes only nodded down the hall toward to the bathroom as he returned to his own seat and plate. The intense concentration over breakfast, along with the beautiful chinaware, gave the situation an unsettling breeziness. They trusted me, or they decided I was too fragile to run after all.

Too fragile to run. That's what my face said when I found it under the lowlight of the bathroom. I'd had my chance and I hadn't taken it. I had let them lure me back inside and now I was trusted to remain there. My face was as my sobs had left it, red smeared and puffy. I unraveled a spool of rough brown toilet paper like a paper bag, and ran it under the faucet before pressing it against my aching eyes.

Over the toilet, a cracked window let in the morning breeze of Stepanakert, along with the sounds of morning birds and the smell of something frying. I pushed on the tilted frosted pane but it opened no further.

I thought of Lucine and the tour group, how my absence might get discussed on the bus that morning. What would Lucine say? I hoped the real estate lawyers would think I'd gone rogue, no more need for guidance or their company.

--

Hovhannes explained what was next. Alisa would drive me in her police car back to Yerevan, back to Eric, back to the domestic life Eric had managed to convince them existed. We'd be there by early afternoon.

"Alisa does not speak so much English but she will see you arrive safe. No problem," he said, slumping back in his dining chair, picking at his teeth.

"Do you expect me to sit in the back of the car like I've been arrested?"

"Of course not, you sit up front."

Alisa blinked. I blinked back.

--

As we buckled our seatbelts I told Alisa I hadn't figured out how yet but I knew she wasn't going to deliver me. I'd make sure of that. Between Stepanakert and Yerevan's city limits, I would figure it out. She, of course, had no idea what I said but on some level it didn't matter.

The sun was still rising as we set off. We passed new color and detail, what the bus had driven by just a few dark hours before. Laundry draped from balconies and tightly clipped shrubs along the grasses of serious buildings. But there was still something sluggish in the air, despite more people on the streets, more cars on the road.

I wondered about the crimes that might be committed in Nagorno-Karabakh. It seemed too still for criminal activity. It seemed like a place whose misfortunes were concentrated in mass conflicts, the residual layers of which clung to the silence in the air.

Leaving Stepanakert, we hit the winding mountains, lined with black forest on the horizon. The mass of impenetrable-looking trees. Alisa slowed down as we passed a monument on the side of a foothill, an old tank covered in white crosses, propped on a stone platform.

"Victory," she said with a broad smile. The first word she had uttered, one of the only she'd say in English.

--

If you Google image search Nagorno-Karabakh, you get a grim pallet. Or, at least I do, with the algorithms assigned to me.

Mostly it's war. Tanks, bombed out and charred structures, men in trenches, barbed wire, the fire of triggered rockets leaving the launcher. It feels curated, the heavy lean toward the colors of human conflict, dingy browns and grays, interspersed with the Kelly green of healthy valley grass. But scattered in I find an old stone monastery, or ancient fortress on a green hill, or that statue—the volcanic stone statue of a man and woman emerging from the earth, the one in Levon's family photo: Papik Tatik. The title translates to "We are our Mountains." It was completed in 1967 and widely regarded as a symbol of Armenian heritage: a man and a woman, half grounded under the earth, atop an isolated hill.

According to the brochure, we were to see Papik Tatik, before making our way back to Yerevan. A quick diversion that would "not be forgotten," according to Lucine. But not seeing Papik Tatik came to symbolize just another way the trip I had set out to compose for myself had been edited by someone else.

--

Alisa stuck to the highway, no diversion to *not be forgotten*. She kept silent and firm, two hands on the wheel, erect posture, self-conscious speed. I wondered if it was me that made her drive such a way. Hovhannes would have instructed it as part of my delicate handling. Or maybe she just didn't drive the mountain roads much.

The break finally came maybe an hour in when she took out her phone and placed it on the dashboard, quickly returning her hands to the wheel.

"Eric," She said softly, nodding to her phone.

She knew his name, as though he were a true person to her. I wanted to tear the car door open, hearing that word, feeling it fill the car, a sour pressure in the air. I ignored her request, cracked the window and let the cool mountain air hit my face.

It wasn't her fault, I knew, but it embarrassed me that she thought it might be what I wanted.

"Eric," she repeated politely.

An idea hit and I pulled Emma's number from my bag before giving enough thought to change my mind.

Alisa looked encouraged, nodding to her phone.

Emma answered on the first ring and I hesitated, almost hanging up at the sound of her chirped hello.

"Emma, I'm in a situation and need some help. Translation help."

"*Of course*, my dear. Bring it."

--

I wasn't sure what to expect of Emma. But she took it seriously when I described the strange place I'd found myself. She jumped on board with that squealy enthusiasm.

Relieved, I handed the phone to Alisa, who took it with hesitation.

I could hear Emma's chirps through the phone and initially Alisa laughed with delight. I bristled. It seemed the world only had one response to Emma. But then Alisa's face changed, eyes narrowed and I sensed her trying to digest something. Emma hadn't held back.

Alisa flipped her words up as though asking for clarification. And then her voice took a deeper tone and I wondered if the two verged on an argument. She hung up after what I feared was too brief an exchange to actually have accomplished anything, placing the phone in her lap.

We continued in silence, through the thick trees and over the switch backs. Alisa's phone would buzz from time to time but Alisa never answered it, never took her eyes from the road, and I knew it was Emma trying to reach me.

After the third or fourth ring, Alisa began mumbling, then her voice rose, went rapid. I didn't turn to look. She was moving through a place where my control ended.

I kept my eyes to the window, but eventually something snapped in me and I cut her incomprehensible speech off. "He has no right to be here."

With my outburst, she got quiet and stayed that way. Hands on wheel, erect in her seat, never taking her eyes from the road. She looked confident. My instinct was to say *I'm sorry you got stuck with this, with me,* but I let it go, my ears popping from the elevation.

--

It was around noon when we came to what looked like a rest stop complex on the edge of a gorge. A cold wind hit as I rose from the car. The gray sky hung low.

"Tatev." Alisa said through the wind, scrambling to pull her hair back. She reached into her pocket, took out her phone and called someone. After some minutes she handed the phone to me.

"Holy shit you're so lucky she took you to *Tatev.*"

Emma's voice cut through the wind.

"Enjoy," she said. "I'm so jealous of your adventure, dear, you have no idea. I haven't gotten there yet. So, listen, she's going to bring you to my house later, I think. You can spend the last couple days in country with me. I had to embellish, said that your husband was abusive."

"But he's not my husband."

"Trust me. If you want me to get through to an Armenian woman, I know what to say. I think she wants you to leave Armenia without such a bad taste in your mouth so she's treating you to a ride on the tram."

"Tram?"

"Okay so I'm going to see you later but dammit go enjoy Tatev. It's the longest tram in the world according to Guinness Book of World records for Christ's sake."

I handed the phone to Alisa. She gave me a long blink.

--

The Guinness Book of World records website has this to say about the tram:

*The longest non-stop double track cable car is 5,752 m (18,871 ft.) and was achieved by the Tatev Aerial Tramway in collaboration with National Competitiveness Foundation of Armenia, in Tatev, Armenia, on 16 October 2010. The tramway, designed by Garaventa (Switzerland), connects the village of Halizor with the secluded medieval Tatev Monastery, offering a spectacular journey across the Vorotan River Gorge. The 5.7-kilometer aerial tramway is supported by three towers between its two terminals. One terminal is on a hill overlooking the village of Halidzor and the other is near Tatev Monastery, on the road to Tatev village. At top speed, the tramway will travel at 37 kilometers per hour and the ride will take approximately 11 minutes, with its deepest drop at 360 meters aboveground.*

I didn't want to ride, wasn't up for getting knocked off the newly determined course of the day. But I didn't want to give Alisa a reason to change her mind, if she was in fact delivering me to Emma, so I let her purchase my ticket and didn't put up much fight when she wouldn't take my money. She was doing it for herself, I determined. She was out for the day, making the best of it. I couldn't blame her.

At 37 kilometers per hour, 360 meters aboveground, passing over the mountain village of Halidzor's red clay roofs and deep green trees, Alisa talked to the car operator, a girl her age, equally pretty and polished. They went on as though they knew each other, as everyone in Armenia seemed to do, or maybe they did know each other. I'd never know.

I focused on Alisa's chatty mouth, her bright smile. She was not the person I had spent the morning with.

--

The day I think of as the day my father really left, I was walking along the main drag that lined the San Andreas Mountains. Wearing his BDU fatigues, he crossed the parking lot of a lounge bar and carried a six-pack of Coors. He saw me before I saw him, approached with lips pressed tight, nodded his head toward his truck, said nothing. I didn't know the F-15s had returned to base. He'd been gone for over a day.

My father drove me to the landing strip. It was the only time I saw his jet up close. As he helped me up into the cockpit's front seat, I smelled the beer on him.

"Here she is," he said with a sigh.

Sitting in the narrow seat, I looked ahead at the console. The black dials and knobs looked delicate enough to snap off if I'd swept my hand hard enough across the dashboard. I wondered how many people around the world had looked up and saw my father in there, flinching as he passed by at 600 miles an hour. I wanted to ask if he had ever killed anyone, if he ever dropped a bomb.

"Looks like a toy," I said.

He leaned away and paced along the side of the jet for a minute, took a bottle of Coors from his fatigues pants pocket and smashed it against the wing.

"We're moving to Germany. I need glasses."

When I asked him to explain what he meant, he leaned down silently and began picking up the shards of glass from the tarmac.

Sometimes I thought of that moment when I needed to remember that nothing can really be frozen. Not even on a canvas or a sketchbook. There is no such power.

--

After a quick meal of kabobs at the Tatev tram restaurant, we continued. Alisa silent, rigid in the seat next to me. I sensed by the hour that we must have been close to Yerevan. And when we finally saw the sign announcing it as 40 km away, my heart began to bang.

Alisa made a call and handed me the phone.

"I gave her my address. So, I have soooo much planned for showing you around Yerevan. And I was thinking you could take a look at some edits I made on my doc. Yeah?"

"Yeah."

Alisa gave me a smile.

Eric would not make it his day.

--

When we reached Emma's building, just after 5 p.m., just blocks off Republic Square, I hovered my finger over the buzzer for apartment 21 B and as Alisa pulled away, I let my hand drop. I wasn't sure if I could bring myself to ring the buzzer to the apartment where I would be safe for the last days of my stay, where Emma would serve as my host, where I would probably meet interesting people, bond with Emma, learn to adjust to her cheer.

I rang the buzzer and when I heard her chirp, told her I needed to go around the corner, pick up something from the convenience store. I'd be right back.

"I'm sure I have anything you would need."

"No, I'll be back in a minute."

"Well let me come with you, hold on."

I walked as fast as I could.

--

Narine told me, "You'll never understand Armenia, but that's just as well."

Narine told me, "It's a safe place, but still you should be careful. You should be careful everywhere. Do not ever not pay attention. Just pay attention and the world will be good to you."

Narine told me, "You can pretend something didn't happen but you can't escape it, because you can't escape time. Things get locked in time with you and they follow you from one minute to the next. And in that way anything can become your story."

Narine told me, "People will want to share their stories with you whether you like it or not so be prepared."

It's embarrassing, looking back to how much of her energy I must have taken in that the few days between deciding to go and doing it brief amount of time.

--

Walking to the square—past the children in their school uniforms, huddles of dehydrated dogs along the curb, old women selling flowers and perfectly made up women—I made my way toward the Marriott, my luggage feeling heavier than it had the entire trip.

But it calmed me, that weight on my back. It was the weight of experience.

I rubbed my stomach and it felt fine. It felt like nothing. I was more than the moments I'd been in.

Soon it would be over. I'd be flying home. I'd put down my heavy bags and with any luck I'd continue to feel the weight of experience. A weight to carry with me and for me only.

I thought about when I got home maybe I'd be able to throw some of that weightiness down. All the weight of my life. Maybe I'd just pick back up those pieces that made sense. Maybe I'd be a little lighter.

But then hadn't that been why I'd shown up? To shed some weight? To unload things?

But still, in that moment, on that walk, it calmed me—that weight on my back.

--

And then there he was, as I rounded the corner to Republic Square, sitting at the Marriott's outdoor cafe. I stopped across the wide road on the other side of the fountain. Even from that distance I felt an uneasy surge. I could tell his head was in his laptop, a sign he was concentrating on himself and not my possible appearance. It was thrilling to watch.

With caution in my step, I made my way a bit closer, slipped into a seat at the same outdoor café I'd visited that first day in Yerevan, and was greeted by the same hesitant server that had served me my first Americano. This time she flashed a brief, bright smile of recognition as she handed me a menu. I ordered an Americano and requested the bill up front, in case I felt a need to make a quick escape.

I took out my sketchbook and began to draw Eric—him and the hotel and the lighting and the patrons that sat all around him. With quickness in my pencil I worked to capture some semblance of the details that made up the world of him in that moment. The light was waning.

A young boy in a school uniform slowed down as he walked by to see what I was doing.

I smiled up and he said something in Armenian.

"I'm just sketching."

"What this?" he said in English, a small voice.

"I'm freezing something here."

He looked at me curiously, working to unlock my words.

I pointed toward Eric, at the risk of catching his attention, and then I pointed to the drawing.

The boy nodded, laughed. "Man," he said, pointing to Eric, a brightness in his voice as though he had just unlocked something.

I ripped the page out of the book and handed it to the boy.

"You go give to him?" I said, pointing again to Eric and then the drawing. "You give?"

The boy smiled and ran off toward the Marriott.

I rose from my seat, steadied the weight on my back, and went the other way.

# About the Author

Heather Rounds is the author of the novella She Named Him Michael (Ink Press, 2017) and the novel There (Emergency Press, 2013). Her poetry and short works of fiction have appeared in numerous publications, including PANK, Big Lucks, Smokelong Quarterly and Atticus Review. Visit her at http://www.heatherrounds.com/

# Acknowledgment

This book was inspired by my travels to Armenia and Nagorno-Karabakh and those I met along the way. I'm indebted to the many people who contributed their time, gave me guidance and shared their stories and histories with me. Some of these people can't go unnamed. Anush Babajanyan, Sona Simonyan, Melikset Panossian, Vahan Tumasyan and the Shirak Kentron NGO, Serli Lala, Sara Anjargolian and Robert Davidian. Thank you to Tatiana Ryckman for her editing genius and to Stevan Nikolic and his team at Adelaide Books for believing in my work. And, of course, Teddy Johnson.

www.ingramcontent.com/pod-product-compliance
Lightning Source LLC
Chambersburg PA
CBHW030830020726
47499CB00006B/2141